Burning Yuletide

Warbler Peninsula series, Book 3

Siobhan Muir

ISBN: 1-947221-06-X
ISBN-13: 978-1-947221-06-2

DEDICATION

Dedicated to J.M. Madden, who writes amazing romance,
and challenged me to write a holiday tale along with her.
Fangirl squee!

.

ACKNOWLEDGMENTS

There are many people who have helped me develop this story and I'm so grateful for their help. J.M. Madden gave me the impetus to write it in time for the holidays and checked over my tale for the proper lingo. Silver James caught my typos and corrected my wordiness (because yeah, I'm wordy). Thanks to Paul Henry Serres for creating the perfect image for the cover and Jerome Laporte for embodying the hero, Mark Redfeather. Great thanks to Kris Norris for adding her creative magic to make the best cover fitting the tale. Y'all rock.

CHAPTER ONE

"There's a hole in my heart. I can't fill it. Can you fill it?"

Mark Redfeather threw his head back and opened his palms to the sky, beseeching the Great Spirit for wisdom and hope. He seemed to have misplaced both after the death of his paternal grandmother. She'd been the sun and the moon to him, the one who had faith in him despite his unusual skillset and talents. Now she flew in Father Sky, always dancing across Mother Earth.

His whole family belonged to the Sky Dancers, the Thunderbirds sacred to the Arapaho of northern Wyoming. He'd been born a twin with his brother Thomas, but instead of a Thunderbird, he'd come out a Firebird, which occurred once in every two million births. A Firebird, the apparent harbinger of a cataclysm that would change the world forever.

He'd never liked that prediction.

His grandmother had taken him in when his parents couldn't handle his propensity to set things alight – the blankets, the house, hell, even the dog – and she'd taught him how to control the tickling flames. He'd learned his true nature and honed his control so he could become the best at his chosen profession.

A firefighter.

The good news was he'd joined a crew of firefighters based in Newberry, Michigan. The air was always damp and the trees almost always wet. The bad news was he often burned hot enough to torch even green wood. And someone was bound to notice a large flaming bird soaring across the night sky.

With his grandmother's death, he felt adrift and lost. He'd thrown himself into work, but even he had to take downtime, and not just because of the regulations. Too bad the downtime allowed him to think and to hurt. The urge to shift into his true form nipped at his control like a yappy terrier.

Tonight, he'd thrown on base layer pants and shirt, grabbed his water pack, hat, and gloves, and gone for a run. He had enough energy to run half the twenty-five miles to Three Lakes, a little town on the shore of Lake Superior. Mark liked Three Lakes, drawn there by energies both powerful and gentle. He'd heard rumors there was a local *Morukai* Shaman, a speaker for the Goddess, living there, but he'd never met her.

Thinking about Three Lakes eased some of the pain from his grandmother's loss and he turned his feet back toward Newberry just as it started to snow hard and thick. Pretty soon he couldn't see more than a few feet in front of him, and he slowed to a jog to conserve his energy. *Fantastic. It's going to be a long run home.*

He tried to stay well off the road as he continued on his way. Nothing like having to call the paramedics to rescue his ass if a motorist slid off the road and hit him. Talk about embarrassing.

As if conjured by the thought, a bright turquoise blue four-door Jeep Wrangler came out of nowhere and skidded to a stop beside him. He jumped aside, hoping he wouldn't get hit if the driver lost more control. But the person inside

2

rolled down the passenger window and called out to him.

"Hey, are you lost?"

The woman's voice held warmth, concern, and a sultry quality that caught his attention in ways he didn't need to be thinking.

"No, ma'am. I'm headed home."

"In a blizzard? Where are you headed?" She shot him a look implying he was crazier than a shithouse rat.

"Newberry."

"That's where I'm going. Can I give you a ride? No one should be out in weather like this, at least not without a car." She leaned over and opened the Jeep's door. "Come on. Get in. It's warm and dry in here."

He debated getting into a strange woman's car, but he'd grown tired of the cold snow dripping down the back of his neck and climbed into her passenger seat.

"Thanks. It's getting nasty out there." He shut the door and turned to offer his hand. "Name's Mark Redfeather." He stopped at his name, struck dumb by her beauty.

Unusually light blue eyes peered out over a slightly beaked nose, arching dark brows, and elegant lips with the corners turned up. From what he could see of her dark hair it rested long, straight, and thick over the chest of her down jacket.

"Pleased to meet you, Mark. My name's Estelle Three-Hearts." She checked her mirrors and pulled back onto the road.

"Three-Hearts is an unusual name. What nation are you from?"

She smiled and it warmed his chest. "I'm half Cree through my mother. So where can I take you in Newberry?"

"I'm headed to the fire station. I'm a firefighter."

Her eyes opened wide and a smile curled her lips, damn near curling his toes. "That's where I'm going. I wanted to talk to your captain about finalizing the schedule for the annual holiday calendar photo shoot. Not much time to get the shots before we sell it for next year."

He raised his eyebrows. "Couldn't you have made a call instead of the drive?"

She grimaced. "I wish. The land lines were down from snow and the local cell tower hasn't been repaired. I had to make the drive because I do better with voice interactions rather than email." She laughed. "I could insult you fifty different ways on email. But in person, I know exactly what to say."

"You're a photographer? Where is your studio?"

"Up in Three Lakes, on the shore of Lake Superior. You folks saved an apartment building there in May."

He nodded. "I remember. Some crazy guy ran into the burning building to rescue a child. I'm just glad the fool got out alive."

"Yeah, I got some great shots of him coming out of the building with her." Estelle gave him a wink. "I sometimes freelance for the local paper." She squinted as they passed the sign to Newberry. "So, you're a firefighter. Are you one of the ones who volunteered for the shoot?"

He hadn't, but after having met the photographer, he'd sign up as soon as they walked in the door. Before he could answer, she squinted at him and smiled.

"I hope you'll volunteer. We don't get many Native American firefighters in the calendars. A lot of women would buy the calendar just to see you. *I'd* buy it for that." She grinned and turned her gaze back to the road.

Why did that warm his heart and harden his cock? He'd literally just met this woman. But he wanted her to look at him, not just as a lovely piece of art to share with others, but also as a man she wanted. *Great Spirit, I want her and I haven't seen more than her face.* And scented her interest.

She wasn't turned on, but she still liked what she saw in her passenger seat.

"I'd be happy to volunteer, Ms. Three-Hearts. Will we be posing with only our equipment or will we have critters as well?" He hoped he didn't have to hold an animal. Most mammals could sense his true nature and did everything in their power to get away. He didn't want to frighten whatever animal they brought in.

"Hmm." She bit her bottom lip in thought and his cock stiffened with the thought of her doing that action in pleasure. "I think for you, I'd have you pose with some of your equipment."

Relief shot through him and he smiled. "That's fine with me. Animals and I don't always get along. Even the station Dalmatian only tolerates my presence."

"Maybe it's just that dog." She laughed.

"Nope. He's not the first fire station critter to warn me off. I don't mind, but I don't want to put an animal in the position of having to hang out with me or getting in trouble." He rolled his eyes. "That's cruel and unusual punishment."

"Oh, a man who's kind to animals. I like that."

Her words set his heart ablaze and the heat raced through him. *Don't flame. Don't flame.* His Firebird self didn't always follow commands, but it seemed to understand showing off all his glory in a small metal vehicle wasn't the best way to impress a woman. *Yeah, because we learned the hard way when I was a teenager.*

Fortunately, they made the turn onto Mulligan Street where the fire house stood and he was saved from having to say more. She pulled up alongside and they both got out. The snow looked pretty coming down in waves through the streetlights, but it piled thickly on the undisturbed ground.

"I love when the snow falls and everything is so peaceful and quiet." Estelle stood for a moment gazing at the snow.

She appeared like a nymph decked out in down jacket, fleece hat, and tall snow boots. Normally, Mark hated the snow and its wetness dampening his fire. But looking at Estelle watching the snow fall warmed him so much he could do so forever.

"Brrr." She shivered and returned her gaze to his. "It's cold enough out here to make my face hurt. Let's go inside."

He'd be happy to warm her up. Preferably as intimately as possible. *Good thing I'm not on duty tonight.* Too bad he had to live in the bachelor barracks at the station. Maybe he'd look for a new place this holiday season.

Mark held the door to the station open for her and watched her ass the whole way inside. He moved his gaze away just as she shot him a look over her shoulder. *But she does have a fine ass.* Round without being bubbled, athletic without being flat. *Sexy.*

As they passed the engine and headed for the rec room, a few of the other team members looked up and interested smiles curled their lips.

"What happened, Redfeather? Did you get lost?" Tommy Atherton snorted until he caught sight of Estelle. "Hello, what do we have here?"

Mark gritted his teeth before he beat Tommy into mulch for looking at Estelle like a Fire Bunny, one of the women who threw themselves at firefighters.

"Lost? No, that's your schtick, Atherton." Mark forced his voice to be even and easy. "And this is Estelle Three-Hearts, the photographer for the holiday charity calendar."

Tommy's eyebrows went up as the other guys got to their feet. "Really? She doesn't look like a photographer."

"And you don't look like a firefighter lounging around in sweats and a wife-beater tank, but I assume because you're here, you probably are one." Estelle didn't smile. "Is the captain in his office?"

The other men behind Tommy nodded and pointed toward the back.

"Thanks." Estelle sailed past them without another look and Mark admired her gumption. She hadn't been that cold to him in the Jeep, but he hadn't suggested she was anything other than who she said.

"Damn, what the hell is her problem?" Tommy shook his head as Estelle disappeared into the captain's office.

"I'm pretty sure it's you, Atherton." Mark rubbed his chin to keep his smile from leaking through. "If you don't want to be treated like a dick, try harder not to be one, yeah?"

He left the guys to add his name to the signup sheet hung beside the lockers. He definitely wanted to be in the calendar. He was perfectly happy to take off his clothes for Ms. Estelle Three-Hearts. Now if he could just convince her to get naked with him. He laughed and shook his head as he signed his name. It would take more than a pretty face to get her affection. Atherton had just proved that.

My kind of woman.

CHAPTER TWO

Firefighters, they're all the same.
Basically, little boys with big toys, and big bodies, running around on adrenaline and caffeine. *And they look at women as more of those toys.* Estelle sighed before she stepped into her uncle's office, reminding herself why she didn't date men who played with fire.

"Estelle, good to see you. What brings you all the way to Newberry on a night with this kind of weather?" Captain Knight looked up from his computer, his white hair sparkling in the desk lamp as bright as moonlight on snow.

"I needed to talk to you about the charity calendar, Uncle Jeff." She strode around the desk to hug his shoulders. "Do you have a moment to talk about it?"

"Sure, sure." He slid his reading glasses up onto his head. "But you could've just called rather than drive all the way out here."

She shook her head as she settled into the chair across from his desk. "The phone lines were down and you know how I hate email. So impersonal."

"You're such a luddite, you know that?" The laugh lines on his face deepened. "So, what did you need to talk about?"

"I need to know the schedules of the men who agreed to come for the photoshoots, find out which have animal aversions or allergies, and what day is good to get the whole crew together to take a group shot. I want to bring in as much money for the Smoke Detector in Every Building program as I can."

Jeff lost his smile as he nodded. "I know this means a lot to you, Flash. How is your brother doing?"

She shrugged, though her heart clenched. "Emery is a little better. His last surgery was in September, but the skin grafts are still really painful."

"Has he been using the lavender essential oil cream I sent?" Jeff's brows lowered in concern. "It really does help with burns and skin wounds."

She shook her head. "I don't know. He doesn't want me to come visit until he's healed up a little more and he was too tired to attend Thanksgiving. I'm worried about him, but his girlfriend says he's doing okay."

Jeff grimaced. "I'm so sorry I wasn't there to help you that night. I was a probie firefighter at the time and was still learning the ropes."

She gave him a smile to make him feel better. "I don't blame you, and I don't think Emery does, either. It was years ago, and we were kids."

"I can't believe he's waited this long to get the surgery."

"He didn't want to, but you know how it goes with money and insurance." She shrugged it away. "It was a horrible accident that could've been prevented if we had detectors, which is why I want to do this calendar." She cleared her throat and straightened her shoulders. "Do you have a complete list of the men who can do the shoot? I honestly only need twelve, but if anyone wants to double up, we can do that, too. Or we can have the same six guys twice. Whatever works."

"Let's go out and check the signup sheet. I think it's as

9

full as it's gonna get." Jeff rose and joined her on the other side of his desk. "Most of the guys weren't all that crazy about finding time to go up to Three Lakes, but we can hope." He held the office door for her to precede him.

"I could always take a pic of you as a hot firefighter Santa. No need for even a beard with that snowy white hair you got going on." She winked and ducked as he playfully swiped at her.

"Only as a last resort. I'm pretty sure most women don't want to see this without a shirt." He gestured to his older, but still trim torso, and she privately disagreed. Older men who stayed in good shape were sexy, particularly to her mature women clientele. Jeff hadn't let the captain's position go to his waist.

When they passed through the rec room, Tommy Atherton had put on a Newberry Fire Department t-shirt and jeans, but Mark Redfeather wasn't anywhere in sight. Disappointment hit her and she blinked a few times to clear her head. Why the heck was she interested in the hot Native American firefighter? She avoided the whole profession. Hell, even her uncle was divorced, the long hours and the thrill-seeking adrenaline junkie mentality not good for long-term relationships.

Though Marilyn wasn't good for Jeff even without the firefighting gig. Her aunt-by-marriage had been one of those firefighter bunnies who wanted the excitement of having a hot guy to show off. She hadn't considered how often she'd end up alone for holidays, anniversaries, and birthdays.

Which is why I don't want a firefighter, either.

She made the thought emphatic as they stopped in front of a bulletin board near the gear lockers. To her delight she had ten names, the last two being Redfeather and Atherton. She wasn't so thrilled with the latter, but the former warmed her heart. There was something about the quietly humorous man she'd picked up in the snow. It would be a delight to photograph him.

"Hey, good turn out." Jeff nodded as he took the signup sheet down. "Will that be enough for the calendar?"

She narrowed her eyes as her gaze settled on him. "It will if you promise to do the hot older firefighter Santa pic." She held up her hands as his eyes widened. "I promise to make it tasteful and handsome rather than the naked-Santa look." She grinned at his frown. "Besides, the older women who buy the most calendars would love it. What do you say?"

"You really think women want to see me without a shirt?" He raised an eyebrow.

She tilted her head and squinted. "Yeah, I'm pretty sure they'd pay extra for December alone."

He threw back his head and laughed. "You got the marketing down pat, don't you, Flash? All right, I'll schedule some time to come in for your photoshoot."

"Good." Estelle nodded, mentally calculating how many more calendars they'd sell as she glanced at the sheet. "Is that name Lucille Engles? I didn't know you had a woman on your crew."

"Yeah, she was a rookie last year, but she's earned her stripes." Jeff nodded, leading her back to the office. "Great firefighter, and she'd probably help you get a few men buying that calendar."

"She's only going on one month, so don't get excited."

They passed back through the rec room, and the men there nodded and smiled, but she didn't return it. She wished Redfeather was present, but he remained scarce. *Dammit.*

Back inside the office, Jeff copied the name list and added their contact numbers so she could call them to schedule shoot times. He also added any animal allergies they'd listed.

"There, that should do it." He handed her the list.

"What about Redfeather's aversion to animals?"

Jeff blinked. "He has an aversion to animals?"

"Yeah, he said he did on the drive here. Something about the station Dalmatian barely tolerating his presence."

"Huh." Jeff tilted his head with a frown. "He's never said anything, but I guess it's true because Sparks never goes near him."

"I'll make sure he's not paired with animals when we do his shoot." She folded the sheet and tucked it into her purse. "I better get back on the road."

"Tonight?" Jeff's eyebrows went up. "Estelle, the snow is coming down hard and heavy. The roads will be damn near impassible. It's not safe, not even for a hotshot driver like you with your 4-wheel drive. Stay here at the station. We have a private room upstairs for families when the weather gets bad."

"But I'm not family—"

"The hell you're not. You're my niece and you need a place to stay. The sheets are clean and so are the towels." He rose from his chair again and shook his head. "There's no getting out of this. If the roads are passible, you can get back to Three Lakes tomorrow."

"But Uncle Jeff—"

"Don't 'but Uncle' me, Flash. Your mother would have my head if I let you drive on a night like tonight, and I'd never forgive myself." He held up a hand to stop her protests. "You're staying the night and that's final. If you're gonna be crazy enough to drive, you can do it in daylight."

He led her down a hallway and up a set of stairs that led to the living quarters for the firefighters. The second floor held another rec room with a foosball table, pool table, and workout equipment for when the crew wasn't watching TV or eating. The third floor had the barracks, a large open room with several beds and footlockers in it. On the left-hand side stood two doors. One led to a bathroom with community showers, and the other led to a bedroom holding two beds and a private bath. The windows looked out over the street outside and the snowy town beyond.

"Here you are. There are fresh towels and other linens in the bureau there." He pointed at an old, beat up chest of drawers. "There's a desk and a charging station there so you can hook up a computer or phone. The Wi-Fi password is Sparks85."

"For the dog?" She grinned as she shrugged out of her coat.

"Yeah, it's in reference to the eighty-five hotdogs he ate at one family picnic. I'd never seen that damn dog poop so much in my life."

"Eww. Thanks for that visual."

"You're welcome. I'm here to help." Jeff grinned. "I'm hoping tonight will be pretty quiet, but people do stupid things when it snows, so the alarm might go off. I apologize in advance. It'll scare you out of bed. Which is the point with firefighters."

"And you thought I'd be safer here than driving home to a quiet apartment?" She snorted. "I think you're selling me short."

"Hey, at least I warned you. Last year, one of the guys had family stuck at the station and he didn't bother to mention the bell." Jeff grimaced. "Shaved damn near five years off his wife's life, and the kids wouldn't quiet down for hours."

"Any loud noises you hear will be my heart galloping for the woods." She waved him out. "It sounds like I better get some sleep when the getting is good. Thanks for the place to stay, Uncle Jeff. I'll try not to soil the sheets when the alarm goes off."

He laughed. "You do that. Have you had anything to eat tonight yet?"

She blinked and tried to think back. "No, I don't think I've had anything since lunch. I've been running around Three Lakes all day."

"Well, hell, that's not gonna work. Come on downstairs and we'll make sure you're fed."

"I don't want to impose..." Actually, she really didn't want to spend much time with Atherton. He gave her the heebie jeebies with his hungry stare.

"Are you kidding? The guys would love to impress the hell out of female company with their cooking skills." Jeff nodded as he held the door for her. "Your things will be safe up here tonight."

She sighed and followed him, glad to see there was a deadbolt on the inside so she could have some privacy. Something about Atherton's stare made her sure she needed the lock.

Too bad Redfeather didn't stare at me like that. No, he hadn't looked at her like something to eat, which would've creeped her out. He'd looked at her with awareness and interest, something she hadn't experienced in a while. *I want to experience it again, as long as it's from him.*

As if the Goddess had heard her thought, Mark Redfeather pulled a long-sleeved t-shirt onto his ripped body just as she stepped into the room. *Sweet glory, he's hot.* His dark chocolate eyes fringed with long lashes took in her presence behind the captain and new interest lit his gaze.

"Hey, Captain. You bringing the photog up here to inspect?"

Jeff shook his head. "Nope. I'm requiring her to stay the night so we don't have to rescue her ass in the middle of a blizzard." He threw her a smirk as she scowled.

"That's a great idea." Mark's lips quirked into a smile. "Although, I would've been happy to escort you home to Three Lakes, Ms. Three-Hearts."

The way he said her name warmed her better than a roaring fire and a cup of mulled cider. She prayed she didn't have a dopey smile etched on her face.

"That's very kind of you, Mr. Redfeather. I'm sure it's

payback for giving you a ride home in the snow." Now why had she said that? She didn't feel like he owed her.

"No, ma'am, but I'm grateful I didn't have to run in it any longer than I did." He nodded toward the stairs. "So, you're joining us for dinner? That should be interesting. It's Atherton's night to cook so you can bet you're going to have something resembling roadkill with a side of potatoes."

Estelle laughed as they followed the captain down the stairs. "Ew, that's not really an image I want in my head."

"At least it's cooked roadkill." Jeff glanced over his shoulder with a smirk. "Not like that sushi shit Nissan made in the summer."

"You gotta open yourself to new dishes, Captain." Mark laughed. "It was pretty good. Almost as good as Rocky Mountain oysters." He shot a look at Estelle and winked.

"Now you're just being gross."

She laughed and several heads popped up out of the rec room and the kitchen, smiles and hope decorating the faces. *Jeez, they're such typical guys.* But Mark lit up and his own smile outshone the others'. *Glory, he's beautiful.*

"Good news, gentlemen. We have a guest at supper tonight, so be on your best behavior and get the food done because Ms. Three-Hearts is joining us." Jeff waved at the guys heading for the kitchen.

Atherton scowled. "Aw, man, and I have to cook, too."

"What's wrong with that, Atherton?" Jeff frowned.

"Nothin', Captain. Just that means everyone else is gonna get to sit next to her while I'm cookin'." He shook his head.

Estelle gave an inward cheer. She'd lucked out. Hopefully, she'd be able to sit next to Jeff and Mark, and be saved from sitting with Atherton.

CHAPTER THREE

Supper in the fire station was usually something Mark looked forward to. The guys were a good crew overall and almost always had anecdotes to keep everyone laughing. But tonight, with Estelle in attendance, it was excruciating. He wanted time with her alone to get to know her better. The drive into town hadn't been enough. And Tommy Atherton power-flirted with her, though Estelle didn't seem to enjoy it much. She smiled when he complimented her or made innuendos, but it didn't reach her eyes.

Unfortunately, it was Mark's turn to do the dishes, but he didn't want to leave Estelle in the same room with Atherton. *What the hell is wrong with me?* He'd never been particularly protective towards any of the women who visited the fire station. But something about Estelle lit his heart on fire, a first in his long life as a Firebird.

Yeah, six hundred years of solitude will make a guy a little jaded.

And now he had to leave the one woman who heated his heart with the biggest player in the bunch. It made him want to chew tin foil.

"You better get to the dishes, Redfeather." Atherton smirked as the others grinned. "I made sure to use plenty for tonight."

Mark scowled as he rose, but it lightened as Estelle rose with him.

"I'll help." She gave him a friendly smile.

"No, no, you sit your sweet tush down, and stay awhile." Atherton sent her a smarmy smile.

"Oh, no, I couldn't. You cooked. I should take a turn to help clean up. That's the way it worked in our house." She stepped away from the table, gathering a few plates as she went. "Can I take your plate, Jeff?"

"Yeah, thanks, Estelle." He narrowed his eyes as he switched his gaze between her and Atherton.

"Great. Gentlemen, if you could pass your plates down to the table closest to the kitchen door, that would help. I'll come back and get them." She smiled as she made it plain that's how things would work.

Mark snorted with amusement as the men hopped-to and he headed for the kitchen to start the soapy water. She'd be the queen of her castle, and the men would be her knights in fire armor just willing to serve. He grinned as he got the dishes started. He'd happily live in her castle.

"What are you grinning at?" Estelle set a stack of dishes beside him and rolled up her sleeves.

"Two things, actually." He moved the plates into the soapy water. "The first is how you outmaneuvered Atherton. He thought he'd get to spend the evening with you while I washed dishes." He chuckled as he picked up the sponge. "I might be juvenile, but it makes me want to do the End Zone Dance every time I think of it."

"That is pretty juvenile." She smiled. "What's the second thing?"

"It was pretty funny how all the guys were tripping over themselves to help you clear the table. Usually, we can't get anyone to do anything except leave everything." He nodded to the pile of dishes. "You got them to stack the plates and gather up the silverware. Nicely done."

She shot him a smirk. "It's a gift."

He laughed and they both dug into the chore. He started to wash while she dried, but in the end they switched because he knew where everything was stored. She didn't seem to mind and he enjoyed the momentary reprieve from washing.

"How did you get into firefighting, Mark?"

Now there was a loaded question. He took his time stacking the dry plates as he gathered his thoughts. Humans weren't supposed to know about the Elder Races, and he was one of the rarer ones. But telling her he had an affinity to fire and a habit of setting things ablaze would ruin his credibility as a firefighter.

"I've always had an understanding of fire since I was a little kid." He kept his gaze on his work. "I knew how it moved and danced, how it cleaned things and renewed things. But as a kid I didn't understand how destructive it could be. It's a natural force that can't be controlled, but must be respected and mitigated. And it always needs a catalyst to start." He shrugged. "I figure I better learn mitigation, using my understanding of how fire dances and feeds to help me protect those who don't."

"That's a good way of looking at it." She tilted her head with a frown. "I like the heat fire provides, and there's something calming about a campfire. But in a building, it scares the living daylights out of me."

"A building is not a good place for fire." He nodded as he reached for the next dish. "Too many things in buildings can feed a fire once started."

"The catalyst you were talking about."

"Yup. Candles, cigarettes, hot iron or curling irons, gas stove left on, electric stove left too long, lightning, loose wiring, kids with matches. And of course, deliberate catalysts like arson."

Estelle nodded. "That's why I'm doing this calendar. I want the Smoke Detector in Every Building program to be a reality. If we'd had a detector in my family home, maybe my brother and I could've gotten out instead of gotten burned."

Mark swung around. "You were burned in a fire?"

She nodded with a grimace. "Yeah. The babysitter panicked and I had to go rescue my little brother. He almost didn't make it, and he's had several surgeries to correct the damage. Only my lower leg got burned, so I haven't done anything about the scars."

"Why didn't your house have any detectors?" Mark kept his hands on the pot he dried rather than gather her into his arms. *She doesn't need my sympathy right now.*

"It was an old house in Detroit with that old '70s carpet, and the wiring wasn't up to code. I think the babysitter was burning a candle, and a piece of paper caught fire. It landed on the carpet and everything went up." She shrugged as if girding herself against the memories. "The smoke detectors either didn't have batteries or shorted out, and none of us knew until it was too late to stop anything. The babysitter was only fourteen and she panicked, running out without Emery. When I realized he wasn't on the front step, I went back for him."

Estelle swallowed hard. "He was okay, but coughing really bad. But the only way out was through the flames and we couldn't get to the bathroom to wet our clothes. He was wearing his dinosaur costume from Halloween, made of flammable polyester, and I couldn't get the flames out when we got to the front door. The firefighters stormed past us and started working on the house, but my brother was burning and I didn't know how to help him. He was only eight."

"I'm sorry, Estelle. I didn't mean to bring up bad memories."

She sniffed hard and shook her head. "It's okay. You would've asked about my burn eventually. And Emery is doing good now. He just had his last surgery and seems to be healing well. But that's why I want to make sure every building in Three Lakes has detectors, so the poor folks in the area can be safe and have a way out before it's too late."

"How old were you?" He put the pot away.

"Ten." She gave him a sad smile. "I know I wasn't responsible for him getting burned, but it made me want to learn all I could about preventing burns and what to do if your clothes catch. And that's why I offer to take photos of people no matter what they look like, to show them the beauty they still have even after injuries and wounds."

"And why you want to do this calendar?"

"Exactly. The money will help get detectors, but the images will remind people of the strength and kindness of the firefighters who are there for them." She smirked a little as she rinsed a big pot. "Not to mention enjoying how you all keep your bodies in great shape. Nothing wrong with that. Gives a whole new meaning to sexy hero."

Normally, being called a hero made Mark uncomfortable, especially with his heritage of being a Firebird. But he understood her perspective, admiring the people who ran into burning places to help others rather than away. And he wanted to be her 'sexy hero' with a desperation he'd never felt in the past.

He laughed and flexed one arm. "I can't argue with that. If you aren't interested in the firefighter aspect, I'm okay with sexual fantasy."

To his delight, she threw back her head and laughed. "You might just get your wish." She winked and went back to work. "Can I ask you a question?"

"Sure." He dried the pot she'd scrubbed.

"I've heard firefighters don't like the word 'hero'. Why is that?"

He stored the pot away as he considered. "I think it has to do with the word itself. 'Hero' means a lot of different things, but most importantly it means squeaky-clean, altruistic, worthy of veneration, pure action without expectation of reward, and most of us don't feel like we fit the bill." He rubbed the dish and set it aside. "We've all done stupid things in the line of duty, or felt like we haven't done enough, or just love the pure rush of adrenaline when heading into a fire. Yes, the end result is we save people or structures, but our motives might not be as pure as the word 'hero' requires, and if the shiny armor doesn't fit, we'd rather not wear it."

"I can understand that. They called me a hero when I went back for my brother, but I was scared the whole time and was afraid of what my mother would do to me if I left him." She snorted. "Not very heroic at all."

"See? Outsiders see heroes, insiders know the truth."

"What truth?" She raised her eyebrows.

"That we're just doing what needs to be done for our own reasons."

She gave him a slow smile. "Yeah, okay. I like that."

The slow smile made his cock perk up and he turned his back before it gave away his appreciation. They finished up the dishes, chatting about mundane things to give them a break from the more personal revelations. He found out her brother lived in Newberry, close to the medical center so he could receive treatment for his burn recovery, but she lived in Three Lakes where it wasn't as busy. Despite the quieter atmosphere, she did a brisk business and a decent living.

"Hey Redfeather, are you done with the dishes yet? You shouldn't make our guest do all the work." Atherton stuck his head in the kitchen door, his gaze locked on Estelle's ass.

Tommy was a damn good firefighter, but Mark found his aggressive flirting style repugnant.

"She insisted. What could I do but give her what she wanted and simply make it easier for her?" He spread his hands in surrender. "But, yeah, we're done. You up for some socializing, Ms. Three-Hearts?"

Estelle smiled, but again, it didn't reach her eyes as she shook her head. "No, thank you. I have to check my email to make sure I haven't missed any new orders for the holidays, and check on my social media business pages. But thank you for dinner and the invitation."

She wiped her hands on the dish towel Mark handed her and headed for the door to the vehicle bay. Atherton paused, blocking her path, and gave her a considering smile as his gaze roamed from her chest to her feet and back.

"How about you come and sit with us for just a bit? We don't get visitors very often at this time of year." He licked his lips before widening his smile.

She stared at him, her expression blank but aware as she considered his request. It took her a long time to answer, long enough that he lost his smile and started to fidget.

Estelle shook her head. "Thanks, but no. I'm going to head up to my room now." She turned to give Mark a small smile. "Thanks for letting me help clean up." Her smile evaporated as she faced Atherton again. "Excuse me, Mr. Atherton. I'd like to go to my room now."

"Sure, I'll escort you up there." He stepped back.

"No, thank you. I can find my own way." She pushed past him and headed toward the stairs.

Atherton turned to follow, but Mark caught his shoulder. "Leave her alone, Atherton."

"Fuck off, Redfeather." He shrugged off Mark's hand. "She's not married and not going out with anyone. She's fair game."

"You don't know if she's going out with anyone, and she's given you all the signs to leave her alone." Mark shook his head. "Hell, her whole body is telling you to fuck off."

"That's not what I'm reading." Atherton smirked. "It's saying 'come fuck me'." He waggled his eyebrows.

"Ew, Atherton. That's disgusting. Leave her alone. She's already said no thanks enough times to you."

"Whatever. You're just hot for her and don't want me sniffing around."

Mark couldn't argue with that, but Estelle didn't seem to mind his company. Atherton wasn't used to being turned down with his pretty-boy surfer good-looks and his firefighter status. But Estelle hadn't warmed to him. If she'd done the same to Mark, he would have heeded her warnings.

He let his face fall into his mask of impassiveness, the one that always unnerved people, and gave Atherton a long look.

"My interest in Ms. Three-Hearts is irrelevant. She told you to leave her alone. Do it, or I'll report you to the captain for harassment."

Atherton reeled back as if he'd been slapped. "What the fuck, Redfeather? What happened to bros before hos?"

Mark gritted his teeth. "She's not a whore, and I'm not your brother. I'm your coworker, and I've seen how you treat women. Not all of them want your style of flirting. She said no. Get over it."

"She only said no because you got in the way." Atherton scowled.

"Seriously? Have you ever considered that you're not her type?"

Atherton raised his chin to look down his nose. "I'm *all* women's type."

Mark gritted his teeth again, this time to keep from smiling. Fortunately, a couple of the other guys had wandered close and overheard him, breaking out in snickers. Atherton whirled and growled as Mark slid past him out of the kitchen.

"All women's type, Tommy?" Mercado chortled. "Alrighty then. The next time the Old Ladies Knitting Club need help with their Holiday Bazaar, I'll be sure to recommend they select you for the duty."

"Yeah, and when the Girl Scouts need help with their cookie drive in the spring, you're all over that, right, Atherton?" Hemsley slapped Tommy on the back.

"Shut up, you know what I mean."

Atherton's frustration with their teasing gave Mark a chance to duck into the captain's office. He wouldn't report Atherton, but something in his gut suggested he needed to warn Captain Knight about Tommy's actions toward Estelle. If a man couldn't hear no from a woman, he shouldn't be near her until he could.

CHAPTER FOUR

Estelle focused her camera on her assistant's left shoulder to get a light reading as the morning light filtered into the front windows of her studio. Today was the first day of the firefighter photoshoot and she was both excited and nervous. After spending the night at the fire station in Newberry, she had a better appreciation for the men and women who made sure to keep her little town safe from flames.

And a better idea of which ones to avoid while they're in the (un)dressing room.

Tommy Atherton was pretty to look at and would make a lot of the women who bought the calendar sigh, but she was more than happy to let them have him. He'd given her the heebie jeebies, and she'd locked the door of the family bedroom upstairs in the fire house just to make sure he'd stay out.

"Okay, looks good, Amy."

Her petite, freckle-faced assistant smirked. "Not compared to what's going to be here in an hour."

Estelle laughed as she helped reposition the light screens. "Don't sell yourself short. You're just as pretty as those heavily built men. And one of the firefighters from

Newberry is a woman."

"Yeah?" Amy's eyes lit up. "Is she sexy?"

Estelle shrugged. "I don't know. I haven't seen her, but I bet she is given what she does for a living. Her name is Lucille Engles, and Uncle Jeff says she's earned her stripes."

Amy nodded as she repositioned some of the hay bales in the studio. "I look forward to helping her at the shoot." Amy hadn't made a secret of her bisexual nature, though she'd never hit on Estelle. "Say what you like. No one is as pretty as a well-built, sexy firefighter."

Estelle laughed. "Except a sexy firefighter with a baby animal."

"Or half naked with a baby animal." Amy winked.

"You're going to have a tough time oiling them up, aren't you?"

"Oh yeah." Amy grinned as Estelle laughed again. "Oh, Hazel said she got the SPCA to bring in a few puppies and kittens." She retreated to the 'costume shop' portion of their studio to check on the props. "She said you'd have to deal with accidents. The kittens should be fine because they're litterbox trained, but the puppies are still young."

"Yeah, I know. I have towels and tarps so it should be easy to clean up." She hoped. The dogs usually left things a mess, but the resulting photos with the firefighters were always worth it. "There are a couple of guys who said they don't work well with animals, so we should probably take those shots when the critters need a break."

Amy nodded. "Okay. Which people say they can't work with animals?"

"Mark Redfeather, Juan Mercado is allergic to cats, and Tommy Atherton doesn't get along with dogs." *Or women, for that matter.*

"What kind of a guy doesn't get along with dogs?" Amy shook her head.

Estelle shrugged as she readied her camera and made

sure all the SD cards were empty. "I don't know. Maybe he's allergic or just had a bad experience with them." *Or maybe they can sense what a jerk he is from fifty paces.*

"I know that look, Estelle."

She glanced up to find Amy standing beside her with a concerned frown. "Who is this guy and why don't you like him?"

Estelle blinked. "I didn't say I didn't like him."

"You didn't have to. I can read it in your body language." Amy crossed her arms over her chest. "What's wrong with him?"

She gave a one-shouldered shrug. "He gives me the heebie-jeebies. He's one of those 'I'm-to-sexy-for-my-gear' kind of guys. He's pretty enough to look at, but his aggressive flirting makes my skin crawl." She forced a smile. "I'm sure he'll be fine at the shoot. And we won't give him a dog to play with."

Amy nodded slowly, but her frown didn't let up. "You let me know if he does anything that freaks you out, okay? You're doing this *pro bono*, and they shouldn't mess that up. The charity is too important."

Estelle gave her a smile. "I know. I'll be professional and not let myself get weirded out by him. Is Hazel going to stay to make sure the critters are wrangled?"

"Yeah, and she's bringing a couple of assistants. Plus, I've invited Jayson Blackamber to help with some of the heavy lifting, and Sheriff Boulderson said he might stop by to see how things are going."

Some of Estelle's tension bled away. "Great. It'll be nice to have so many helpers. We're supposed to have six out of the eleven names here today. I think we'll be able to get them all done as long as the critters don't cause too much hassle. But you know what I always say."

"Yup. Expect the unexpected."

"Right. We have to balance the need to get the photos with the firefighters' work schedules. And reshoots, etc."

Estelle rubbed her face with her hands. "It's going to work out, but it might take a lot of flexibility."

Amy bent in half and grabbed her ankles, turning her head to look at Estelle. "Like this?"

Estelle laughed. "No. Stop showing off. Not all of us are a yoga master."

Amy straightened and winked. "Hey, someone has to attract all those firefighters. You didn't see one you liked?"

Estelle kept her lips sealed as she made sure her camera was cleaner than clean.

"Oh, ho ho. Who is he? I assume it's a he. Have you met him already or did you just see a photo?"

Estelle rubbed the back of her neck. "Yeah, I met him when I went down to Newberry to talk to Uncle Jeff. I picked him up on the road. He was jogging in the snowstorm."

"Oh, good. Someone just as crazy as you." Amy grinned. "I didn't think it was a good idea for you to drive that night, but I take it back. So, is he handsome?"

"What kind of a question is that? Of course, he's handsome, a little taller than me, and broad shoulders. He had nice legs, too."

"Nice legs?" Amy raised her eyebrows. "When did you get to see his legs?"

"I told you, he was jogging. He had on those thermal leggings, and they showed off all his muscles." Estelle shivered with exaggerated pleasure. "I'm telling you, he has superhero thighs."

"Glory help us, you and your love of superhero thighs." Amy mock-rolled her eyes.

"It's no different than your love of buxom blondes." Estelle shot her a dry look.

"Yeah, okay, I might resemble that comment. Is the lady firefighter blonde?"

Estelle laughed. "I don't know. We'll find out later today."

"Yes, we will." Amy winked before she headed back to make last minute preparation for their incoming firefighters.

Estelle rose and made sure to check everything again. The lights, the camera, the light screens, the props, everything to make the shoot go smoothly. But her mind kept going back to the quiet, humorous man with the chocolate brown eyes and long inky black hair. She hadn't seen the hair until he took off his hat at supper that evening, but he'd kept it braided and rolled into a bun at the back of his neck. What she wouldn't give to take that hair down and run her fingers through it. *Glory, it would be better than a little girl's slumber party.*

Along with the hair, he was just beautiful. Broad shoulders, flat belly, clean shaven face, and those chocolate eyes worked perfectly to star in all her hot man dreams. He even had a voice with the sound texture of smooth chocolate. And his laugh? Glory be, she melted into a puddle every time she heard it.

As if her mind had conjured him out of the either, Mark Redfeather strode into her studio like a warrior ready for fighting fires. He carried his turnout gear with him, but wore the helmet for convenience. Her mouth dried out and her heart hammered in her chest at the sight of him. Then he smiled, and her knees went weak.

Sweet glory, I want him.

The thought took her totally by surprise. She hadn't been interested in men since her last boyfriend decided she was too damaged for him, whatever that meant. He'd known where she came from and what had happened with her little brother. But the moment he saw her burn scar, he'd run for the hills and stopped answering her calls and texts. The last communication she'd had from him was a text that read: *You're too damaged for me. We wouldn't have worked out anyway. Thanks.* She'd written off all men at that point.

But Mark Redfeather bypassed all her natural defenses with just a smile. *I'm in so much trouble.*

"Hello, Ms. Three-Hearts. How are you today?"

Hot, horny, and happy to see you?

"Good, thanks, Mr. Redfeather. Are you ready for your shoot?"

He paused with a grimace. "Not hardly, but I can face burning buildings. I'm sure I can handle this."

She lost her smile. "If you'd prefer not to have your picture taken, you don't have to. This is purely voluntary."

"It's not the photo, it's the undressing." He tilted his head. "I don't like to be naked in front of a large audience."

"Oohhh." She nodded and rubbed her chin. "We could always have you leave your t-shirt on. As long as we can see your arms and the muscles in your chest, it'll be fine."

"Yeah?"

"Yeah. If the model is uncomfortable, the camera will catch it and the pictures come out mediocre." Her smile returned as his shoulders relaxed. "We'll just have you in your t-shirt, turnout pants with suspenders, and helmet. That should work great."

"All right, then. I'm good with that."

"Aw, what's the problem, Redfeather? Worried your chest is too flabby?" Atherton sauntered in, a smirk curling his lips.

"Nope, I just don't want to make the rest of you look bad." Mark lost his smile, but his expression remained subtly amused. "I'm just doing this to help Ms. Three-Hearts and the SDEB program."

"And we thank you very much for your help." Estelle let her smile grow warm. "We've had a few outside donations, but the calendar will put us in the black. So, let's get to it. Mr. Atherton, I think we'll do you first."

"Now, that's what I like to hear." He winked at her as he strutted over to the changing area.

Estelle rolled her eyes and shot Amy a look. She

grimaced, but nodded. *Get used to it. Firefighters are as cocky as SpecOps guys.* She checked her camera for a few more moments before she focused on the other firefighters who'd come in.

Lucille stood with Juan, Mark, and another firefighter Estelle hadn't met yet, while Atherton got dressed. Amy helped him get ready, but refused to oil his skin. She let him do that himself. He teased her about manly muscles, but Amy gave him a perfunctory smile and handed him the oil.

"Ready, Mr. Atherton?" Estelle called as her studio doors opened and another man came in. "Please come sit on these hay bales while Hazel gets you a kitten." She glanced at the newcomer. "Hey, Mr. Blackamber. Nice to see you."

"Good to see you, too, Estelle. Still need some help?" Jayson Blackamber ambled into the room and everyone seemed to straighten. He had the kind of power and magnetism that got people's attention fast. *It's just because he was a Navy SEAL.* That quiet predatory energy followed them whether they currently served or not.

"Yes, please help Amy adjust the lights and move the bales. And I think we have a bench with the truck backdrop."

"Will do." Jayson moved to help.

Atherton sauntered back to the studio floor in his turnout pants and little else. "You want me right here?" He settled onto the nearest bale.

"Yes, set your helmet beside you and rotate your legs to the right." Estelle shifted into her professional photographer mode, no longer focusing on Atherton as a person. "That's it. Hazel, do we have a kitten?"

The director of the SPCA in a nearby town brought a cute black and white tuxedo kitten to Atherton. He took the thing with trepidation as if afraid he would crush it. The kitten dug its claws into his pants and mewed, but

31

otherwise didn't move much.

"Good, now turned more toward the camera, but keep your gaze on the kitten."

"Like this?" The man shifted one leg down while his big hands kept the kitten from sliding off his pants.

"Yup. Just right there. Good." She snapped a few images, from different angles. "Okay, maybe hold the kitten up? Good right there. Hold still." She snapped more pictures.

She flowed into a rhythm of directions and camera clicks, with Amy adjusting the lights when she needed it. Despite Atherton's periodic leer, he responded very well to direction and seemed to enjoy playing with the little cat.

"All right. I think we got it, Mr. Atherton. You're free to change. If you need to shower, there's one in the back bathroom." She waved the man from her set.

"You sure I can't convince you to join me?" Atherton winked at Amy, but she frowned.

"Very sure. I have other firefighters to work with." She tilted her head. "Unless you don't know how to wash yourself?"

He snorted, but some of his bravado left while the other firefighters chuckled. Estelle shot a look at Mark and caught the end of his eyeroll, but he smiled when he met her gaze.

"All right, who's next?"

Lucille stepped into the set. The woman had short, dark hair and sharp green eyes, but her smile came easily enough to form deep laugh lines around her mouth. Hazel's assistants gave her a couple of puppies, one husky and one shepherd. The dogs settled around her and made her laugh, which made for beautiful images. Amy grinned the whole time, her eyes alight with pleasure and attraction. Lucille noticed the attention, but appeared shy and kept her focus on the dogs. Estelle found herself grinning as much as the other two women.

"Excellent. You look great, Ms. Engles. Thank you. Who's next?"

Juan Mercado came next and she had Jayson remove the hay bales and add the bench as they dropped the firetruck backdrop into place. Juan played with the shepherd puppy and the dog warmed to the man quickly. Estelle caught their delightful moments with her camera, absorbing their joy as much as their beauty. Juan's darker skin looked great against his yellow pants with red suspenders and the dog looked at home with him.

"You should really consider adopting Felix, Mr. Mercado." Hazel clipped a leash to the dog's collar when the shoot ended. "I've never seen him warm up to anyone like he does to you."

"Are all the dogs up for adoption?" Mercado shot a look at Estelle.

"Yeah, it's a joint promotion. The sale of the calendar goes to help the SDEB program, but all the dogs and cats photographed will be available for adoption over the holidays." Estelle pulled out the SD card and replaced it with a new one. "Hazel and I have been working together for years."

"And it always benefits both of us." Hazel grinned. "Plus, I buy the holiday Firefighter calendar just to enjoy it. Because of the animals, of course." She winked and grinned while Estelle laughed.

"Oh, sure, you do." Estelle waved at the next firefighter. "Come have a seat. Which do you prefer? Kittens or puppies?"

The man ended up with one puppy beside him while two kittens sat in his upturned helmet. He had a nice chest and large nipples that pointed down. Estelle found him handsome and friendly, but her gaze kept shifting over to where Mark stood watching everything with Lucille. She wished he was comfortable with taking off his shirt, but she understood his sense of privacy. Maybe she could get everyone to clear out and just get a few shots of him shirtless.

Glory, I'd like him to be completely naked. But not in front of her camera. *What the hell is wrong with me?*

She finished with the last man and rotated her head on her neck as Jayson and Amy brought in a fireman's ax and a coiled hose. They placed them in front of the truck backdrop and arranged them artfully. Amy had a wonderful eye for setup, more of a perfectionist than Estelle herself. *Thank goodness I have her.* Atherton tried to help as a way to attract Amy's attention, but she didn't respond beyond a polite 'no thanks.' Estelle bit her lips to keep from smiling. She checked her camera and SD card, then raised her head.

"All right, Mr. Redfeather. I'm ready for you." *Glory, am I ever.*

She might have said the words, but what appeared in her view was far more than she expected. He'd removed his shirt, but he wore his yellow turnout pants with red suspenders and a matching red helmet. She damn near swallowed her tongue when he met her gaze and smiled.

Hard muscles covered his chest and belly with only a small line of hair leading down into his pants from his bellybutton. Healthy copper skin glowed in the lights and showed off an intricate tattoo on his left shoulder and arm. It looked like the flames coming off a bird, and her mind immediately thought of the Firebird stories her grandmother had told her while they cleaned fish for their Thanksgiving feasts.

"Where would you like me to stand?"

In my bedroom with nothing on.

She cleared her throat and narrowed her eyes as if to determine the best light for him. *That would be any light at all.*

"Stand with your hand resting on the butt of the ax and one foot up on the bench." She had no idea where the directions came from as her mind had checked out. He moved as she'd asked. "Yes, right foot. Good. And rest your right arm on your thigh while you rest your left hand on the ax." He moved again and she held up her camera to hide the drool pooling at the side of her mouth. *Holy glory, he's sexy.*

She snapped a few shots, directing Amy to move the light screens a little here and there. Then she had Mark move the ax up to his left shoulder and smile at the camera. A few of the others made snarky remarks and he laughed, brightening up the shots.

"Okay, we're almost done. Now I want you to stand facing me, arms at your sides, and head turned to your right."

Mark positioned himself just as she'd asked, but something wasn't right.

"Amy, can you take down one of the suspenders? The right one, I think."

Amy raised her eyebrows, but Mark allowed her take the right suspender off his burly shoulder. A lovely coppery nipple appeared where the suspender had hidden it, and Estelle wanted to suck on it while she ran her hands over his belly. *Focus, Stel.*

"Good. Yeah. Okay one last thing. Drop your head forward, spread your feet about shoulder width apart, and hold your arms out just a little, as if you're going to bend down to pick up the coiled hose."

He moved into the position with a few adjustments and she snapped images like it was going out of style. The light perfectly caught the shape of his jaw and nose under the helmet, as well as the muscles along his sides at his ribs. She enjoyed the view through her camera of his exposed nipple and the tattoo. *That's it. Perfect.*

She reluctantly dropped the camera, knowing he'd cover up his lovely body again.

"All right. You're done. Thank you, Mr. Redfeather."

Mark raised his head and met her gaze. Amusement

and something else swirled in his chocolate gaze, but he looked away too quickly for her to decipher it. He pulled the helmet off his head and unpinned the braided bun at the back of his neck. His glossy black hair fell to the middle of his back in a thick braid and she wanted to slide her hands over it. *And not just the braid.*

Damn, she was definitely horny. She'd have to spend some time with her vibrator that night.

Mark retreated to change into his street clothes while Amy and Lucille helped Hazel crate up the critters. Juan helped with the dogs and spoke with Hazel about the possibility of adopting Felix the shepherd. Jayson and the other firefighter moved the props to the side so they'd be easy to use the next day when the rest of the firefighters would be back for the other half of the shoot.

Mark returned to the main studio dressed in jeans and the Newberry FD t-shirt. He looked very good, but she'd liked him without his clothes, too.

"Thank you for taking the time to volunteer, Mr. Redfeather. It was a pleasure working with you." She tried to keep it professional while the others stood within earshot.

"For me, too, Ms. Three-Hearts." His smile warmed her more than it should. "You made it so easy and relaxed. I was worried I'd be too stressed to do it, but you made it fun."

"What made you decide to take your shirt off?"

He frowned. "You didn't like it?"

"On the contrary. I liked it a lot." She leaned closer and lowered her voice. "You would've looked good anyway, but I think you're very sexy in your helmet and pants."

He stilled and she raised her gaze to his, trying not to inhale the scent of him. He smelled of Mesquite wood and clean sweat, and she wanted to spend her days snuggled up to him. Her thoughts made her pull back and take a deep breath to calm her heart.

"Sexy, you say?"

"Yes, sir." She smiled even as the heat flared in her cheeks. "I'll definitely include you in the calendar. Maybe for my birthday month."

"Which is?"

"January."

He raised his eyebrows. "So, your birthday is coming up?"

"Yup. She's a New Year's baby." Amy winked as she walked by.

"Really? A New Year's baby? That's lucky."

"She even got a story in the paper that year. She was the first one born at the stroke of twelve." Amy grinned. "You should show him the article. First baby born at the start of the new decade. It was a big deal."

"It's not a big deal anymore. We had a new millennium since my birth. I'm pretty sure that baby got far more attention than I ever did." Estelle waved away Mark's surprise. "So yeah, you will get to lead off the calendar year."

He grinned. "I'm good with that. Turns out, I'm a New Year's baby as well."

She blinked. "You are?"

"Yup." He winked. "I knew there was something I liked about you." He tucked his helmet under his arm as he turned to go. "I'm going to take this out to my truck, then I'll come back in here to help clean up."

"Oh, you don't have to—"

But he was already across the room at the door.

"So, when do we get to see these pics?" Atherton leaned against the desk with her computer. "Will we be able to get prints?"

"I haven't decided if I'm going to release the prints, but I might make them available to the models. You can definitely buy a copy of the calendar, Mr. Atherton."

"You sure you don't want a poster sized one of me? I don't mind." He leered at her and she swallowed back bile.

"Only if she plans on throwing darts at it, Atherton." Juan clapped him on the shoulder and grinned to take the sting out of his words. "Glory knows there will be plenty of image to hit your fat head."

"Shut up, Mercado." Atherton scowled, but there was no heat in his voice. "You're just afraid she'll notice how fat your head is."

"It's not my head that's fat." He playfully winked at Estelle as he ducked Atherton's swipe. "Come on, *cabrón.* Let's get back to Newberry. You owe me a game of foosball."

"You mean an ass-kicking." Atherton sauntered out after his friend.

"Yeah, keep talkin', bad boy. Put your money where your mouth is."

Their conversation faded as they stepped out of her studio and she breathed a sigh of relief. She didn't like Atherton, but at least Mercado could keep him distracted. *And he's not coming back tomorrow.*

Nor would Mark Redfeather. Sorrow pinched her gut and she turned away to hide the urge to bend in half. Why did it matter? She'd just met him. It wasn't like he was being deployed to some far distant part of the world. He lived only twenty-five miles from Three Lakes.

Shaking her head, she sat down at the computer to start downloading the images from the SD cards. She'd look at them after her studio was put to order and she'd had some supper. The shoot had taken most of the day and she'd forgotten to eat despite the lunch stuff Amy had brought in for the firefighters.

"Do you need me to come back tomorrow, Estelle?" Jayson paused at the front doors.

"Yeah, is that okay? I really appreciate the help."

"Sure, not a problem. Kate says hello, by the way.

She's planning to buy one of these calendars for the hot guys." He rolled his eyes, but grinned. "But after seeing that woman firefighter, I might be tempted to buy one as well."

Estelle laughed. "Won't the guys at your job give you side-eye for having a calendar full of mostly naked men?"

Jayson snorted. "Maybe it will give them something to aspire to. Besides, the puppies and kittens are damn cute. See you tomorrow."

"See you, and thanks, Jayson."

He pushed the door open and headed out just as someone else stepped in. Estelle didn't have to turn her head to know who it was. Her heart thundered and her nipples tightened into peaks as Mark's presence filled the room.

"What can I do for you, Mr. Redfeather?" She gave him a warm smile.

"First, you can call me Mark." He rested a hip against her desk as he looked down on her with those smoldering chocolate eyes. "Second, you can let me take you out to supper for your hard work today. You were amazing."

She raised her eyebrows. "Are you asking me out on a date, Mark?"

"Yes, ma'am, I am. I'd like to spend some more time with you."

"You were with me all day today." She saved the downloaded images into a folder and shut down the computer as she returned her gaze to his. "You haven't had enough?"

"Not hardly." His eyes flared with arousal. "And I wasn't really with you all day. I watched you work. There were too many other people here to be 'with' you."

Heat curled through her chest and she shivered. "How did you want to be 'with' me?"

He pulled her to her feet with one hand then brought it to his lips to kiss. The heat of his lips against her fingers sent pleasure shooting straight to her groin.

"To be brutally honest, I'd like to see what you look like without a shirt." He grinned. "But I'll settle for supper at a local place, my treat."

"Was it so bad to be without a shirt?"

"Not with you taking the photos. As I said, you made it fun."

"I'm glad you enjoyed it. You made the images look fabulous. It'll be fun editing them."

He raised his eyebrows. "You edit them?"

"Of course, for light, color, exposure. Some of them I make black and white just to see the shadows." She nodded as she stood. "It's how images look so good on book covers, calendars, and gallery shows. Without the enhancement, the originals are often really dull."

"Oh, I didn't realize it took so much work." He stepped back to let her pass and followed her has she tidied up the last little things before she turned off the lights. "I thought it was all about the focus and light to start with, and once it was shot, it was done."

"I wish. Thank goodness for Photoshop. It makes the job easier." She headed for the coat rack set beside the costume rack. She was tempted to take one of the prettier jackets, but it wouldn't keep her warm in the December Michigan weather. "Where do you want to go for supper?"

"Isn't there a little café here that everyone likes?"

"The Ironwood Café? Yeah, the food is great. Iris and Ben Maple run it. Nice people." Estelle shrugged into her down coat. "She always dyes her hair. It's great. You never know what color it's going to be."

"Really? She sounds very cosmopolitan for the Warbler Peninsula." He zipped up his own coat and threw a wool beanie on his head. "Let me get the truck warmed up and we can go."

"All right."

She watched him duck outside into the dark evening. It

was only after five, but the daylight had fled and it seemed much later. Mark started his truck and the headlights showed flakes of snow falling through their beams. *Great, another snowstorm.* She hoped the other firefighters had made it to Newberry without too much trouble.

"Hoo-boy, it's cold tonight." Mark returned to the studio, stomping his feet.

"Pretty rough out there, huh?" She watched the snow fall for a short time. "We can skip the Ironwood Café and head to my place. It's not far and wouldn't keep us out in the snow that long."

A smirk curled his lips. "Are you inviting me back to your place?"

Heat skittered through her at the idea of having Mark all to herself. But then she thought of cooking and dishes, and shook her head.

"On second thought, I don't want to do dishes tonight."

"Is this payback of having to do dishes the other night at the fire station?" He held the door to the studio open for her.

"Maybe." She winked before she pulled the door shut after him and locked it. "Wouldn't you rather just have someone else cook and clean for you?"

"Hell yeah. Not a requirement, but definitely a plus." He led her through the snow to the truck and opened the passenger door. "Get in and stay warm. It's face-hurting cold again tonight."

She laughed as he shut the door and walked around the front of the truck. He seemed to glow in the snowy light, the flakes disintegrating on his shoulders the moment they touched him. *That's because he's so hot.* She giggled at her thought as he climbed into the driver's seat.

"All right, where am I headed?"

Straight to my heart. She pointed out the window. "North and east. That way."

"Okay." He backed the truck out of the parking stall

and turned onto the road. "You know, you avoided my question of inviting me back to your place."

"I didn't avoid it, I simply chose not to answer." She grinned as he chuckled. "But yes, I'd like you to come back to my place after supper. Given how much snow is falling, I think it might be a good idea anyway. I don't want you to crash this nice truck on the drive to Newberry." But she remembered his job. "Unless of course you're on duty tomorrow."

"Nope. I have tomorrow off as well. I thought I'd get some laundry done."

"Exciting."

"Oh yeah." He laughed as he turned the truck onto Main Street.

Three Lakes had decorated for the winter holidays with lights strung across the road from lamppost to lamppost. The soft white light made the whole town sparkle and she loved driving under it. In the snow, it looked like a winter wonderland.

"I love this town."

"Do you?" Mark grinned. "It's got good energy for sure. If I didn't have to be at the fire station so much, I could see settling here."

"Yeah?" She sat up a little straighter, the idea warming her more. *Get a hold of yourself. You've just met him.* "There's the Ironwood. They have parking around back if you don't find anything on the street."

Fortunately, someone with a truck the size of Mark's pulled out and they were able to take the spot right in front of the restaurant.

"Well done. You must lead a charmed life."

The gaze he dropped on her made her shiver with its intensity. "I definitely do, especially since I've met you."

Before she could respond, he ducked out of the truck and headed for her door to open it for her. His words surprised and excited her. Something about the way he'd said them suggested he liked the change and wanted more. *I definitely want more of him.* She didn't normally fall for guys so fast, but Mark's warm calm hinted at a banked fire and she wanted to touch the heat.

I want to touch a lot more than that. No question, but she schooled her expression to hide her inner thoughts as he opened her door and helped her out of the truck. Maybe she'd get lucky that night.

CHAPTER FIVE

Mark didn't want to release Estelle's hand once she'd gotten down from his truck, but he didn't know how she felt about such public displays of affection, and forced himself to release her. She smiled in gratitude as they headed for the Ironwood Café's entrance and he basked in her pleasure.

He'd meant it when he said he could move to Three Lakes. The energy was good here and he suspected it had a lot to do with the *Morukai* Shaman residing in town. The werewolf who'd helped with the hay bales in the studio carried the energy signature of someone far older and more grounded than his apparent age. He made a mental note to ask Estelle about him.

Stepping inside the Ironwood Café gave the impression they'd arrived at a winter forest, albeit a warm one. Trees appeared to make up the support beams and booth posts within the room. Thick needle foliage made up of spruce, fir, and pine covered the ceiling and white lights hung from the boughs. The calm atmosphere helped settle some of his internal fire, but he reminded himself to be extra careful. He sensed the beams belonged to living trees, but he could still cause them damage.

It's not a good idea to piss off a Dryad in their own Garden.

"Where do you want to sit?" Estelle tugged on his arm as she gestured around the room.

"How about in the booth against the wall?" He started for it, preferring to have his back to the kitchen. Something about the night's energy made him want to sit facing the door.

"Okay." She smiled as she wound through the room to the booth then shrugged out of her coat. The booth post had little stubby branches especially good for hanging coats and scarves.

As they settled into the booth, a tall, willowy woman wearing a festive green and red headscarf stopped by the table to hand them menus.

"Welcome to the Ironwood Café. What can I get you to drink?"

"Hey Iris. I think tonight I'd like some hot tea, herbal please." Estelle gave her a warm smile.

"Hot tea, got it." Iris matched her smile before turning her gaze on Mark. Her expression turned wooden. "And for you?"

She's a very powerful dryad. Mark tried to make himself non-threatening. "I'll have some coffee, please."

She narrowed her eyes a moment before a perfunctory smile curled her lips. "Tea and coffee. Alrighty. I'll be back in a bit with those."

Mark watched her go and wondered if she could tell what he was. Estelle still didn't know and he wasn't sure he could tell her. *If you want to be with her long term, you're going to have to mention it.* Yeah, it would be hard to hide a huge flaming bird on the days he needed to shift. It was a bit too early to reveal his dual nature, though.

"How long have you lived in Newberry, Mark?" Estelle pulled her hat off and set it beside her. Her dark hair shimmered in the white lights.

"About ten years. I came because they needed firefighters who didn't mind the cold."

"Oh, yeah, you definitely have to have thick blood to live up here."

"How long have you lived in Three Lakes?" He settled back against the booth and enjoyed the way her face animated when she spoke.

"Ever since I graduated from college with my bachelors in art. The photography professor said he'd visited this little town up on Lake Superior that was so funky. His words, not mine." She shrugged. "We took a field trip up here and I was smitten. After living outside of Detroit all my life, this place seemed like a paradise. I moved up here as soon as I could afford the U-haul truck."

Iris returned with the drinks and a warmer smile. "Here you are. It's good to see you again, Estelle. How is the charity calendar shaping up?"

"Great." Estelle beamed as she gestured to Mark. "Mark Redfeather is one of the Newberry firefighters who's volunteered to be in the calendar. We did our first shoot today."

Iris's gaze warmed almost as much as her smile. "No wonder you're so handsome." She laughed as the heat crept up his face. "Have you met Kate Blackamber yet?"

Mark shook his head. "No, ma'am."

Estelle nodded. "I haven't met her in person, but Jayson said she wanted to get one of the calendars when they're done. He helped with the heavy lifting in the shoot today. And Mark was one of the firefighters who helped with the big apartment fire back in May."

"Oh, yes." Iris nodded, her gaze sharpening on him. "Were you part of the crew who manned the donation table at our holiday festivals?"

He nodded, grasping the cup of hot coffee. "I was here for Memorial and Labor Days, but I couldn't make the July Fourth festival."

"Hmm, and you haven't met Kate?"

"I don't think so."

"Hmm." Iris shrugged and her smile smoothed out. "I'm sure you'll get a chance while doing the photoshoot. Kate's a huge supporter of the SDEB program. No one wants to see fire destroy the town." She shot him another intense look and he had a feeling the dryad woman knew his heritage.

"No, ma'am." He'd gotten the subtle warning, and wondered why Kate was so important for him to know.

"Are you ready to order or do you need a few more minutes?"

"We'll need a couple of minutes." Estelle tucked a loose tendril of hair behind her ear.

"Okay. I'll be back in a little bit."

Estelle watched her go, a little frown lowering her brows. "What was all that about?"

Mark shook his head. "I don't know. But you know how little towns are when someone new stops by. I'm sure she just wants to make sure I'm not here to cause trouble." *Especially since I'm a Firebird sitting in the middle of a living forest.* Yeah, the dryad woman might be a little nervous.

"It was weird. But I've heard of Kate and she's a big shot around here. Kinda like the mayor without all the political weirdness." Estelle shrugged as she perused the menu. "Maybe Jayson will bring her with him tomorrow to the shoot."

Big shot, huh? He wondered if Kate was the *Morukai* he'd heard of. If Iris pushed him to meet her, he suspected every member of the Elder Races new to the area needed to check in with her. Being vetted by the local Speaker of the Goddess let the other members of the resident Elder Races know who to trust and who to watch out for.

By the time Iris returned, they'd made their selections and placed their orders then settled down with their respective drinks.

"So, tell me about where you're from." She sipped her tea.

"How do you know I'm not from around here?"

"Seriously?" She snorted. "You have western nation written all over you. Which nation are you from?"

"Arapaho, from Wyoming." The loss of his grandmother returned and he had to swallow a few gulps of coffee to keep it from leaking out of his eyes. "My grandmother recently passed."

Sorrow devoured her smile as she reached for his hand. "I'm so sorry, Mark. Blessings to you and your family."

"Thanks. It hit me hardest because she raised me. In fact, the night you found me on the road, I was trying to clear my head after her loss."

"Oh glory. So it was recent."

"Yeah."

"Wow, I had no idea. Are you going back to Wyoming for the memorial?"

He shook his head. "No. I can't leave. Our schedules are too unpredictable."

"Horse shit." Estelle frowned. "I'm sure my uncle will give you the time off. Family is important."

"Your uncle?" He raised his eyebrows.

"Yeah, Captain Knight. He's my mother's younger brother. I'm sure if you ask, he'll give you leave to go mourn your grandmother."

That explained a lot. He'd wondered why she seemed so familiar with the Newberry fire department despite living in Three Lakes.

Mark smiled and nodded. "I'll think about it. It hit me pretty hard and I haven't been able to process all of it. Heck, I haven't even talked to my brother about it yet."

"You have a brother?" She tilted her head. "Is he handsome like you?"

Mark damn near spit the coffee across the table. "Uh,

yeah, I guess."

She raised her eyebrows. "You guess?"

"We're twins. So, if you think I'm handsome, you'll probably think the same of Thomas."

Sweet Goddess, don't let her meet Thomas. Of the two of them, Thomas had been the ladies' man, his quiet ease attracting women left and right. Mark had always been too shy and too afraid he'd let loose his fire to be very charming with his brother around. He'd grown up since then and found his own stride with women, but he still faded into the background when Thomas was in the same room.

"Twins? Wow. Is he in Newberry, too?" She looked hopeful and he tried not to let it eat away at his confidence.

"No. He's in a little town in Colorado with their Hotshot team there. Why?"

"Because having sexy firefighter twins would've been great for the calendar." She gave him a warm smile that made his cock perk up.

"You still think I'm sexy?"

She opened her mouth to answer, but Iris returned with their supper orders and they paused their conversation. They thanked her and Estelle waited for her to move off before she said anything, but it wasn't the answer he was looking for.

"This looks good and I'm starving."

Disappointment speared into his chest, but he smiled and nodded. "I can imagine. You didn't stop moving once today."

She shrugged as she dug in. "Once I get going, I'm kinda in a zone and I forget about things like food or rest."

"Tomorrow we'll have to make sure you eat, then." He grinned as she raised her eyebrows.

"You're going to be there tomorrow?"

"Yeah." He gave her a shrug, ignoring the roar of the flames in his ears. "If you're okay with that. It's my second day off and I don't mind helping out."

"Oh, yeah, that would be great." Her smile warmed his heart. "And for the record, I think you're really sexy."

The roar of jubilation from his inner Firebird surprised the hell out of him, but he grinned and thanked her before they tucked into their food. Their conversation turned to lighter subjects, but he rode the high of her admission and barely remembered anything they talked about.

He paid for their meal at the front of the Café and Iris took his money while Estelle used the bathroom.

"You need to check in with Kate Blackamber, Mr. Redfeather." She ran his card and waited for the print out. "All the Elder Races need to meet her. It's how we keep ourselves and her safe."

He raised his eyebrows. "I don't have any aims to hurt anyone. I'm a firefighter."

Iris nodded, the beads on the end of her headscarf tinkling. "I understand, but we've had trouble with folks showing up here with nefarious intent. Kate herself has been threatened a couple of times. It's just how we do things here. Do you know what the word *Morukai* means?"

He nodded as he signed the credit card receipt. "Yes, speakers of the Goddess."

"Yes. That's Kate, and we do all we can to make sure she's safe. So new Elder Race members need to visit with her." Iris took the receipt. "Will you be coming back to help out with Estelle's photo shoot tomorrow?"

Mark nodded as Estelle returned to the foyer. "Yes, I've promised to be the muscle to move props around."

"Jayson said he'd come back, too, but it's always good to have more than one person to move everything around. It makes the shoot go smoother." Estelle zipped up her coat and stuffed her hat on her head.

"I'm sure it'll be great with both of you to help." Iris nodded as she set the receipts aside. "Maybe Kate will come with Jayson and bring some of her famous cookies to share."

Mark narrowed his eyes, suspicion running through him, but Estelle groaned with pleasure.

"That would be awesome. Of course, I'll get fat off her cookies, but I'll enjoy it." She grinned as she stuffed her hands in gloves. "Thanks for supper, Iris. Tell Ben it was excellent as always."

"Will do." Iris waved with an innocent smile as they left the café, but Mark didn't buy it.

I'll bet Kate Blackamber will be at the shoot tomorrow because Iris makes sure of it.

CHAPTER SIX

The snow had fallen hard and fast while they were in the café. It lay up to her knees as she trudged to Mark's truck.

"Wow. That's a lot of snow." He clicked the automatic start and the truck rumbled to life.

"Yeah, it is. It's been a long time since it's fallen quite this fast." She loved the look of the snow in the lights of town, but it had become damn near whiteout conditions. Even with 4-wheel drive, it would be stupid to drive very far in this weather. *Maybe I can convince him to stay with me.* For safety, of course.

Right.

"Give it a minute to warm up and then I'll drive you back to your studio."

"Okay." She bit her lip, not quite ready to ask if he wanted to stay. It was fortunate her apartment sat above the studio, making it easy for her to get to work. *And for him to stay.* She shivered in pleasure at the idea.

"Are you really cold? You can wait inside the café until the truck's warm." He stepped back to open the café's door for her.

She shoved her hands into the pockets of her down

jacket. "That's okay. Out of the wind will be good enough. Aren't you cold? It's freezing out here."

He shook his head as he opened the truck's door. "I have an internal furnace." He grinned and winked. "Climb in. It won't take long to warm up."

She didn't waste time scrambling into the passenger seat.

"I'm going to clear the snow from the front and the windshield while it warms up. Stay inside and warm."

"What about defrost?" She brushed the snow off her thighs.

"That button, there." He pointed before backing out of the truck and closing the door.

She hit the button and cranked the fan on high as he slogged to the bed and opened a container behind the cab. He managed to brush the majority of snow off the hood and windshield before he retreated and grabbed a shovel. The snow had grown deeper while he worked, but at least the front windows cleared with the heat blasting the glass.

At last he climbed into the cab with her and gave her a bright grin. "Wow, it's deep. Let's get you to your studio before it gets impossible to move."

She nodded and fastened her seatbelt as he eased the truck into the street. Fortunately, they didn't have to turn around, but the plows hadn't been by for a little while and the going was slow. Visibility made them inch along toward the lake and they only discovered they'd reached the Lake Road when the headlights lit the two-ended arrow caution sign.

"Guess we have to turn left here, yeah?" Mark raised his eyebrows.

"Please. I don't feel like going swimming tonight."

"What? This is the perfect night for it."

"Yeah, if you're a polar bear or a harbor seal."

Mark's rich laugh echoed in the cab as he turned the wheel and crept toward her studio. Thank goodness she'd left the front lights on. It was the only thing that made her building visible in the whiteout.

"Turn right there between those two cars." She pointed to their left. "There's a parking lot behind the building that's pretty well shielded by big pine trees. That's where my Jeep is."

"All right."

He slowly took the turn and she thanked their lucky stars no one else was crazy enough to be driving tonight. He stopped the truck beside her Jeep and threw it in park before he turned to her. She studied the lines of his face from the sensual mouth to the deep chocolate eyes under dark arching brows, and she wanted more time studying them.

"Well, here we—"

"Come in and stay the night, Mark." Her words tumbled over his in a rush, and her face heated.

He blinked. "You want me to stay the night at your place?"

"Yes. Yes, please." More than she'd wanted anything in a long time. Something about this man with his quiet confidence and his sexy body made her want to keep him near her. "It's late and the snow is coming down hard. It's safer for you to stay." Safer? Not hardly. She'd have to fight to keep from throwing herself at him. "Please. I don't want to worry about you driving back to Newberry tonight."

He nodded slowly, his expression thoughtful. "All right. Do you need anything from your studio or your Jeep before I take you home?"

Estelle shot a look at the building. "Oh, glory. I never told you. I am home. I live above the studio in an apartment upstairs." She bit her lip. "Sorry. I forgot you don't come here every day."

"Not a problem. It's convenient." He grinned as he turned off the ignition. "All right. Let me pull the wiper blades up and we can go in."

They both got out of the truck and Estelle dug through the snow on her Jeep to pull up her wipers while he extended his. She lost sight of him as he returned to the bed of his truck, but he reappeared and followed her to the front of the building.

The door to the apartments on the second and third floors stood between her studio and the shop next door. She punched in a code and the lock disengaged. They hurried inside before the wind blew in more snow. She realized he carried a duffle bag with him when she closed the door behind him.

"I'm on the second floor, first door on the left." She pointed at the stairs and followed him up, enjoying the view of his ass in his jeans. *I'm terrible.* But she didn't feel very guilty for savoring his male beauty.

"This is a nice old building. It's pretty close to the one that burned in May, isn't it?" He paused at the landing so she could catch up to him.

"Yeah, only two blocks. It was crazy and scary. But the community was great and jumped into action while they waited for you to arrive." She pushed past him up the second flight of stairs to the hallway. "Iris set up the triage tent and the whole town pitched in to help."

"It was surprisingly organized when we arrived, I will say that." Mark nodded as he followed her to the door. "Thanks for the place to stay tonight. I didn't really want to drive back to Newberry."

"I didn't want you to drive back, either." But not for the reasons she'd mentioned. She really wanted the opportunity to get to know him better without all his crewmates with him. *Glory, I hope he feels the same.* She unlocked her door and pushed it open. "This is home. Come on in."

She'd loved the apartment the first moment she saw its old "distressed" wood floors, white plaster and lathe walls, and stained wood accents on the doorways and baseboards. She'd decorated with plush rugs of neutral colors to hide the dirt, and bright throws on the hand-me-down couch and chairs. All her furniture was of the garage-sale variety, but it all seemed to work, and she liked her little home.

The kitchen and dining space looked out over Harbor Lake while the living room had a real brick fireplace on the wall between her unit and the one behind her. She loved lighting it and letting the cheery fire heat her house instead of the furnace, which rattled and hummed like a grunge band from the 1990s. While the apartment had two bedrooms, she'd converted one to a personal office/meditation room where she could practice yoga after she'd sent emails and interacted with clients.

"Go ahead and put your bag anywhere. I'm going to change. Then we can make a fire." *Too bad I can't make a fire with him.* She shook her head and headed for her bedroom as Mark took a look around. *I gotta rein in this horniness. It's been way too long.* She hurried to her room before he caught her blush.

****

Mark stopped by the front door and hung up his jacket as well as removed his boots. He liked her home. Her choice of décor created a chic and homey effect, and her added holiday decorations with lights and pine boughs made it festive. He had no problem staying here tonight. Even better, the way she'd aligned her home fit the natural energies within the town. Without trying, she'd connected to the magic within the world.

"Go ahead and put your bag anywhere. I'm going to change. Then we can make a fire."

Oh glory, she'd already made a fire in his chest by her invitation to stay, and his cock rose to meet it. The idea of her changing into something else had him clenching his fists in resistance to the urge to follow her. *Stay put.*

"Do you want me to start a fire? I'm good at it." He headed over to the brick fireplace and his Firebird settled a little with the scent of charred wood.

"Yeah, okay. That would be great."

She'd stacked chopped firewood in a bin beside the hearth and even had natural wood shavings for kindling. He squatted beside the opening and built a respectable mound of wood and shavings before he shot a look at the hallway. The room remained empty. He sighed and released a little of the fire inside him toward the hearth. Flames, golden and hungry, leapt from the piled wood, crackling with joy as they worked on consuming the fuel.

"Wow, that was fast."

Mark jumped and turned. He hadn't heard her come back into the room and hoped she hadn't figured out how he'd started the fire. *What the hell am I doing here? She's human.* And he wasn't, no matter what guise he wore while amongst them.

"Yeah, the kindling must have been extra dry." It was a lame excuse, but he didn't know what else to say. 'Hey, I'm a Firebird so I got this' was out of the question.

"Yeah, I try to keep it in a box so the damp doesn't get to it." She smiled as she rubbed her arms in a fleece shirt that molded to her curves. "Brr. I'm still cold. I'm going to make some tea. Would you like some?"

He blinked a few times, his gaze stuck on her nipples pushing at the shirt. Damn, they were more beautiful than he thought. He hadn't noticed them while she was working and the first time he met her she'd been wearing her down jacket. But now they were in perfect view and they teased him with their perkiness.

"Mark?" She looked down. "Do I have something on my shirt?"

He felt the heat rise in his cheeks as she looked back up at him. "Uh, no, nothing on your shirt."

She smirked. "Were you looking at my nipples?"

He rubbed the back of his neck under his braid, not sure how to respond. "Yes, ma'am."

"Do you like them?"

Her question made him blink in surprise. "Yes, ma'am."

"Good. Want some tea?"

"Yes, ma'am."

She grinned and turned to the kitchen to set the kettle on to boil. Her frankness delighted him and he ambled into the kitchen after her, a dopey grin curling his lips. "You're not offended that you caught me staring at your chest?"

"Nope." She pulled out two mugs from the cupboard. "I wanted you to notice."

"At risk of losing all hope for more, why?"

She turned her head and dropped her chin. "Because I'm hoping for a lot more than just supper and conversation tonight."

His jaw dropped. "Really?"

"Yes, really. Unless you'd prefer to sleep out here on the couch by yourself." She shrugged as she gestured toward the living room. "I do have a comfortable couch and some great pillows and blankets. Probably enough to make a blanket fort."

Mark tilted his head. "I only want to make a blanket fort if you'll join me in it. Otherwise, I prefer the bed."

Estelle laughed. "I'd join you in the fort, but I prefer the bed, too. Especially if you're thinking about more than sleeping in it."

"I wasn't before, but I am now." Despite the playfulness of their conversation, Mark didn't want to overstep. "Are you sure you want this, Estelle? I don't want to screw anything up if we go too far too fast."

She frowned, tilting her head. "Don't you want to have sex with me?"

He groaned. "Hell yeah, I do. But I don't really like

one-night-stands. I tried them a few times, and they left me cold. Particularly if I really liked the person. And I really like you. I don't want this to be a one-and-done sort of thing."

The smile curling her lips warmed his heart more than the fire in the hearth. "I really like you, too, and I'd like it to be more than a one-and-done. But we've only known each other a few days. Are you sure you want more?"

"Yes." He didn't elaborate. He didn't need to. His Firebird knew what it wanted and he'd learned from experience that once it made up its mind, it was a done deal.

She laughed. "Are you sure? You sounded hesitant there." She grinned through her obvious sarcasm as the kettle whistled on the stove. "What kind of tea would you like?"

He needed something to rein in his raging cock, but he looked over the boxes of tea she pulled from the cupboard. "Something herbal. I'm already revved up enough tonight."

She dropped two green tea bags into the mugs and poured the water before heading into the living room to enjoy the fire. He followed like a dog on a leash, the need to be close to her calling all the shots. He'd never felt that way about anyone, but Estelle Three-Hearts captured his attention and attraction like no one else.

They settled on the floor in front of the fire and he gripped his mug tightly to keep from grabbing her and pulling her sweatshirt off. Those perky nipples teased him with their stiff little points and he wanted to suck on them to see if she was as sweet as she smelled. *Get a grip, man.*

He jerked back from her when he realized he was leaning in close, and the tea leapt out of his cup onto her sweatshirt. *Shit!* She shrieked and jerked away, spilling her own tea on her pants. She shot to her feet, yelping in pain, and he joined her, helping her rip off her sweatshirt and pants.

Caramel colored skin glowed in the fire's light combined with a neatly trimmed vee of curls between her legs, and Mark's brain short-circuited. Estelle hissed and stepped out of her clothes, the sleek muscles in her legs and ass bunching as she moved. Mark forgot to breathe. *So beautiful.*

"Shit." She hissed as she took note of the red marks on her skin. They weren't large or bad, but he bet they hurt.

"Do you have any lavender oil?" He headed for her bathroom to distract himself from perusing the rest of her glorious flesh.

"Lavender oil? What for?" Her voice filled with pain as she grabbed her clothes and followed him down the hallway.

"It's good for burns. It helps heal the skin without scarring." He ducked into the bathroom and opened the medicine cabinet as she kept going down to her bedroom.

"I think I have some in my bedroom. I use it for the diffuser to help me sleep."

That made sense. He turned off the light in the bathroom and headed for her room, only to stop dead. She sat on her bed, bent over so her full breasts hung below her chest, spreading oil on her leg where he'd dumped his tea. Despite the minor injuries, he wanted to kneel at her feet and touch all the glorious skin she offered him.

"Here, let me help." He managed to kick his brain into gear.

"I've got it." She capped the little lavender bottle and set it aside, a frown drawing her brows.

"I'm very sorry." Mark knelt at her feet anyway and met her startling light blue gaze. "I didn't mean to drop my tea on you. I lost my balance,"—partially true, not that kind of balance—"and tried to regain it too fast. I'm sorry."

"It's okay. I got most of the clothing off before it burned me." She tilted her head and narrowed her eyes. "Or was that your whole plan? Get me naked?"

Her suspicion made him laugh. "Well, yeah, but not quite that fast. And I'm not a fan of burns. It's my job to make sure they don't happen." He leaned forward to kiss her knee and she gasped in surprise. "I'm so sorry, Estelle, for accidentally dumping my tea on you. Let me make it up to you." He turned his head to kiss her other knee, inhaling the delicious scents of lavender and sandalwood.

"You smell divine, *beebeenei*." He murmured the word for beautiful in his native language against her inner thigh.

"It's the lavender oil." She shook her head as he slid his hands over her warm thighs.

"I smell more than lavender." He raised his head to meet her gaze as he massaged her skin with his thumbs. "Let me give you pleasure, Estelle, to make up for the tea."

He held her gaze, hoping she'd let him sample the sweetness he could smell between her legs. He wanted to make her forget her worries and the sting of the burn so he didn't destroy any hope of connecting with her. Because he needed her in ways he didn't understand, and didn't want to question.

CHAPTER SEVEN

Mark's gaze held hers and Estelle couldn't look away from the fire behind his eyes. Like the deadly element, it drew her with its heat and appearance of life, and she remained transfixed.

Let me give you pleasure, Estelle. That's what he'd said and she couldn't say no. And why should she? He was handsome, sexy, and so virile she couldn't believe he was interested in her. *Yeah, not gonna say no.*

"Okay." Eloquent she was not, but when he kissed his way up her thighs, she no longer cared.

"Lie back for me, *beebeenei*, and spread your legs." He sat back far enough to pull off his shirt and she couldn't help but stare at his beautiful body as it came into view.

She loved the heavy pectoral muscles above the ridged abs, but the thick muscles on his arms and shoulders took her breath. The firebird tattoo on his left arm tempted her to lick its lines, but he winked at her as he unbuttoned his jeans, loosening them for the hard ridge of flesh behind the zipper.

"Lie back now." He rested a warm palm on her belly and pushed gently. She followed his instruction and settled onto the bed. "That's it. You're very sexy, *beebeenei*."

"What does that word mean?" She met his deep brown gaze and shivered with the heat she read in them.

"It means 'beautiful', which you are, Estelle." He knelt up and spread her legs a little wider. "I love to look at your pussy with the hair all trimmed. Do you prefer it trimmed or did you do it for a lover?"

"I trimmed it once for a man, but realized I liked it that way, so it's all for me." She gave him a smile. "I'm glad you like it."

"Oh, I do. It lets me see your lips and clit very well." He leaned forward and licked her from her slit to her clit without dropping her gaze. "And you taste so damn good."

The slick, wet heat of his tongue against her sensitive flesh stole her breath and the strength in her arms. She flopped back onto the bed with a moan as he settled in to feast on her. He drew her legs over his shoulders while he leaned into his task, humming with pleasure.

Reaching over her thighs, he peeled her nether lips apart and teased her clit out of its hood with his tongue. Erotic, tickling pleasure shot through her body as he scrubbed her flesh with his tongue's tip. She whimpered and rocked her hips to the slow, measured strokes on her nether lips.

"Oh, glory, Mark. That feels so good." She fisted her hands in her bedcovers, the pain from her mild burns fading into the background.

He hummed his approval as he massaged her clit with his thumb while he inserted his tongue into her slit. Exquisite heat hit her senses as his tongue trailed along the walls of her pussy and she rocked her hips again, wanting, needing to get closer. She hissed her pleasure as he thrust his tongue in and pulled out slow, teasing her with hints of what was to come.

When he moved his mouth to her clit and sucked hard, she wailed as the erotic sensations shot straight to her brain, making her see stars. Her orgasm built with each pull on her clit and she rocked her hips to get closer. Estelle squeezed her hands in the covers to keep from grabbing his head as he licked her slit. Her pussy tightened and cream flooded her channel, making him moan.

"Yes, Mark, lick my pussy. Glory, lick me."

He did so much more than lick when he slid a thick finger into her slit and sucked on her clit. Her orgasm shot closer and she rocked her hips in time to the thrusts of his hand. She keened in supplication for more. *Glory, he needs to give me more.* More sucking, more licking, more thrusting. Anything to propel her closer to the release just out of her grasp.

As if sensing her thoughts, Mark thrust another finger into her clenching pussy and growled against her sensitive clit. Sweet pressure built as his fingers shuttled in and out of her, but when he curled them inside and hit that special spot, she saw stars.

Her release exploded through her like a comet, leaving a trail of pleasure. She wailed her ecstasy out as she flew with her orgasm. Mark hummed and moaned along with her, feasting on her release with abandon. A red-gold firebird streaked across her vision as the pleasure trebled and she soared with it, joy following in its wake.

When she came back to her body, she found her lover settled in beside her on the bed. She had no memory of them moving up to the headboard, but she liked having his hot body beside her. He stroked the skin of her breasts as her breathing settled back to normal and she turned her head to meet his glowing gaze.

"Thank you."

He grinned and waggled his eyebrows. "Thank *you.* You're glorious when you come."

"Am I?" She snorted, but a smile curled her lips. "Good to know. That's not what my last lover said."

Mark raised his chin. "Your last lover was an idiot. You're beautiful, and your current lover thinks so."

"That would be you?"

"That would be me." He leaned over and sucked one of her nipples into his mouth. He immediately moaned. "Sweet Goddess, I've wanted to do that since you came out wearing your sweatshirt."

She grinned. "That's why I put it on. I didn't expect you to get me out of it like that, though."

He laughed, but his expression filled with chagrin. "I'm sorry about the tea. Does it hurt much now?"

She shook her head. "Nope. I can't feel a damn thing beyond pleasure." She glanced down their bodies at his still encased in denim. "I think I need to repay you in kind."

"Oh yeah?" A sexy smile curled his lips. "And how do you propose to do that?"

"Take off your jeans and I'll show you." She rolled onto her side, her orgasm still throbbing through her as she watched him work his jeans off his hips along with his boxer briefs. "Glory, I love the shape of your thighs."

He dropped the jeans off the bed and settled back, his cock thick and hard, curving toward his belly button. She did love the shape of his thighs with their light dusting of hair, but they only highlighted the beauty of his cock and balls. He'd trimmed his pubic area, leaving enough darkness to remind her of the treasure she sought.

"Oh yeah, you're fucking gorgeous." She knelt beside him as she stroked her hands down his ridged belly to his straining penis. "I want to suck on your cock and taste you. Fair's fair, right?"

"You don't have to, but I won't tell you no." The smile broadened into a grin as his deep chocolate gaze tracked her movements. "If you want to suck my cock, I'm all for it."

"How do you want me to suck your cock?" She tilted her head as she trailed her fingers around his scrotum, watching his cock flex and his balls tighten. "Soft and slow? Hard and fast? A little of both?"

"Are you offering me choices?" He wiggled his hips a little, letting his hard cock wave. "Surprise me."

"I like your style." She leaned over him to run the tip of her nose along the crease between his scrotum and thigh, enjoying the musky male scent. "I want to take my time and not rush things."

Mark groaned and his eyes slitted, but he kept his gaze focused on her. "Oh yeah, take your time. I'm good with that."

Yes, he is. His cock flexed in her grip as she dipped her head and slid her tongue around the edge of the glans. A bead of pre-cum hit her tongue and filled her mouth with a salty, smoky flavor that had her taste buds aching for more. *You can't taste just one.*

She slid her mouth all the way over his flared head and down his shaft until the tip hit the back of her throat. Then she swallowed.

"Oh, sweet hell, you're killing me, Estelle." She'd never heard that much strain in his voice before, and she liked it.

She hummed with his rigid flesh in her mouth and he moaned in response, arching his back. She slid up his shaft and licked around the head with the flat of her tongue, before shoving it back between her lips. She sucked on the smooth skin of his shaft then raked her teeth over the edge of the glans.

Mark whimpered and rocked his hips as she tightened her mouth around his flesh. She trailed her fingers over his sac and he moaned, rocking harder. Excitement seared through her at her ability to drive him crazy with pleasure. She'd rarely been willing to give a man a blowjob, but she'd wanted to taste Mark since she saw him half-naked in her photography studio. She wasn't going to give up this opportunity.

Again, she took him deep into her throat and swallowed, but instead of groaning and taking the pleasure,

Mark grasped her shoulders and pulled his cock out of her mouth.

"Aww." She pouted as he pulled her closer to his body, his breath sawing in his chest.

"Oh, there's no way I'm gonna come down your throat tonight, *beebeenei*."

He kissed her hard, thrusting his tongue into her mouth. He tasted of tea and that smoky flavor she'd sampled from his cock. *Curious.* Definitely delicious.

"I want you to ride me tonight, Estelle."

"Ride you?" She pulled back so she could meet his gaze. "As in on top of you?"

"Yeah." He reached between them and grasped his hard shaft. "I want you to take control and pleasure yourself as much as you pleasure me."

She scanned his eyes, excitement building. She'd never been given the opportunity to ride her lover. All her previous partners wanted to control the lovemaking. The idea of setting the pace thrilled her.

"Do you have a condom?" She rocked her nether lips against his hard shaft.

He groaned, throwing his head back and closing his eyes. "Ah, glory. Yeah, in the back pocket of my jeans."

She rolled away from him, careful not to touch his straining cock as she fished the foil packet out of his jeans. "Do you want to do the honors, or shall I?"

"Please. I'm not sure my fingers will work at this point."

"So easily overcome. I didn't expect that of a firefighter."

He opened his eyes, fire burning behind the brown irises with a warm glow. "Only with you, *beebeenei*. Only with you."

Estelle tore open the package and kissed the tip before she smoothed the latex over his straining shaft. He hissed as she ran her hands over him, squeezing his balls gently.

"You're very sexy, Mark." She crawled up his body to straddle his groin. "I'm going to enjoy this." She grasped his cock and positioned it at her nether lips before she sank down on him.

****

They both moaned as her slick pussy engulfed him to the hilt. *Sweet Goddess of Flame, she's fuckin' hot and tight.* He fought the urge to move and tried to enjoy the taut, wet heat of her sheath wrapped around his dick.

"Oh, glory, Mark. You're so thick." She shuddered as her pussy tightened around his flesh. She licked her bottom lip. "Glory, you feel so damn good."

He couldn't agree with her more. He raised his hands to her hips and gently lifted her a little, pulling his hips back. His cock tugged against her grasping walls with reluctance, as if she didn't want to let him go. *Never let me go,* beebeenei. The words echoed in his head, and some small part of him realized he meant them.

Then she moved.

The sweet, tight drag of her pussy over his dick liquefied his thoughts until only she remained. He couldn't speak, couldn't think. All he wanted was more. More of her scent, more of her taste, and more of her sweet, hot pussy grasping his cock.

She rose and fell with a slow roll, her sheath tightening around his shaft with a drugging sweetness. He wanted to tell her to take her time, to go slow, but he couldn't find the pathway to push thought to voice. The pleasure of being deep in her body and watching her take joy from him made coherency impossible.

I want her forever. He shouldn't. He wasn't human, not even remotely, but he wanted her and only her from now until the sun's fire consumed the planets. He wouldn't be settled or at rest until she was at his side.

"Oh glory, Mark. I need you. I need you so bad." Estelle whimpered as she rode him harder, her full breasts bouncing on her chest. "I'm going to come so hard around your cock. Oh glory."

Her words and her motions set his orgasm in motion and he could do nothing about holding back. Not when her pussy clamped down hard on his shaft and her inner walls fluttered around him in an erotic massage.

Ecstasy shot through him as he threw his head back and roared his joy. Her own cry of bliss mixed with his and he sailed on it, his release boiling from his balls. His Firebird screeched its jubilation and a little lick of fire snaked from his fingers to her hip, scorching a small silhouette of a bird on her skin.

She moaned and came again, her pussy clamping down on him with the force of her pleasure, and he soared with her. *Mine. She's mine.* He ran his hand over her branded skin, but she didn't flinch and the skin remained smooth.

They settled back into the bedroom and he opened his eyes to find her staring down at him with a slumberous gaze.

"Hi there."

"Hello." His voice sounded breathless even to him.

"That was wonderful."

He nodded. "It was."

She slid to the side and peeled the condom off him. "I'm going to clean up. Don't go away, now."

"No, ma'am."

He watched her ass sway as she headed for the bathroom and let a smile curl his lips. He was no stranger to sex, but what he'd shared with Estelle was so much more than a simple release. He'd accidentally bonded to her and now he had to tell her what it meant and what he really was.

Dread hit him in the chest and drained his pleasure. He'd made a spiritual and emotional connection to a woman who knew nothing about him, at least nothing about what really mattered. He had to tell her.

But when she returned to the bed with a warm washcloth and a smile, the words stuck in his throat and his courage failed him. She was human and humans had no clue the Elder Races existed in their world. For the most part, it had kept the Elder Races safe from human fears.

"There. All clean." She tossed the washcloth into a laundry hamper and snuggled up against him, her soft skin and scent calming him. "I'm so glad you stayed here in Three Lakes tonight, Mark."

"Me, too." He kissed her forehead and she sighed with contentment.

He wished he could feel the same.

I just bonded with a human. And he couldn't tell her because if she found out, she'd run screaming from him. But it was a bell he couldn't unring.

Holy shit, I've really fucked up.

CHAPTER EIGHT

Morning came with a hot man in her bed and a thick blanket of snow outside. Estelle hadn't felt so relaxed and cozy in a long time. *That might be because I also haven't had sex in eons.* She couldn't argue and didn't want to. Hopefully, her drought of sex was over.

She didn't want to get out of bed, but the other firefighters would be arriving in a little over an hour and she had to be prepared. She raised her head and stared at the beautiful man asleep in her bed. *This is what I want every morning.* She snorted, shaking her head. *Yeah, like that's gonna happen.* Although he did say he'd wanted more than just a one-night-stand. *Me, too.*

Mark took a deep breath in and opened his eyes, his gaze finding hers unerringly.

"Good morning." She leaned her head on his chest.

"Good morning." His lips curled into a semblance of a smile. "You're beautiful."

That was a first. No one had ever told her she looked beautiful first thing in the morning. The compliment made her heart flutter.

"Thank you. So are you." She rubbed her cheek against the smooth skin of his pectoral. "What does your tattoo mean?"

He blinked as if trying to marshal his thoughts. "That tattoo is my totem, the spirit who watches over me and protects me. It's a Firebird."

"The harbinger of a cataclysm that's meant to cleanse the world in purifying fire?"

He sighed. "That's the one. Though I prefer to think of it as the fires of renewal that promotes growth, burning away the old and decaying bits of negative energy."

She let his words sift through her consciousness, remembering the odd dream she'd had the night of the fire in her childhood home. She'd seen the Firebird, rising up toward the ceiling in a wash of flame. But instead of breathing its fiery breath down on her and her little brother, the great bird had extended its wing to make a path for her to escape. It didn't last long, but she'd taken the fire-free corridor to save herself and her brother.

"I can see that. I thought I saw the Firebird in a dream once. It showed me the way out of the flames to safety."

He raised his eyebrows. "You saw a Firebird?"

She waved her hand with a smile. "It was a dream, but it didn't feel threatening. More like a protective guide."

"I could see that. The Firebird has been couched in threatening roles forever, but they're more of a fiery protector, fighting demons with their own weapon." His gaze turned intense and she shivered as his voice deepened. "Never believe the Firebird would harm you deliberately, Estelle. His only goal is to protect you."

Energy fluttered through the room as if a vow had been made, but when she turned her gaze back to Mark, he yawned widely and rolled his sexy body out of bed. "I'm going to shower."

"Okay." She tried not to be disappointed with his departure. They did have to get up soon. "I'll go make coffee." It didn't stop her from watching his tight ass saunter to the bathroom, though.

Hell no, I'm not going to turn down such an opportunity. She scrambled out of bed and threw on her robe as she headed to the kitchen.

It didn't take him long to shower and by the time he came into the kitchen, the coffee was ready. She handed him a cup with a kiss on the cheek and headed for her own shower. Despite the sweetness they'd shared in bed, he'd withdrawn a little, and it worried her that maybe she'd said something insulting about his totem.

When she came out from getting dressed, Mark wasn't in the apartment. She frowned and looked out the windows to a world of white. The snow had accumulated deeply around the vehicles and lamp posts outside, though the plowing crews had cleared most of the road. She looked for Mark on the street, but remembered he'd parked his truck in the back lot. *He's not planning to leave without saying goodbye, is he?*

The thought chilled her to the bone and she returned to her kitchen to pour some coffee in her travel mug. *Please tell me he hasn't left.* She hadn't thought she was that bad in bed. Maybe she hadn't pleased him? But she remembered him crying out in pleasure to shake her rafters—and probably her neighbors'—after they came together.

Just as she'd worked herself into a tizzy, someone knocked on her apartment door. Mark appeared through the peephole and she breathed a sigh of relief, laughing a little at herself.

"Hey, I'm glad you came back."

Mark raised his eyebrows as he stepped over the threshold. "Of course, I came back. Why wouldn't I?"

She closed the door, a blush warming her cheeks as she shrugged. "I don't know. When I didn't see you in the apartment I thought maybe you were headed back toward Newberry, and…" She trailed off with a grimace. "I don't know."

She expected him to laugh at her fears, but he chose to step close and wrap his arms around her. "I'd never leave without saying goodbye. And after last night, you'll never be rid of me."

She frowned a little at his wording, but her fears melted away. "Okay, good." She pulled back and dropped a quick buss on his lips. "There's hot coffee and I have an extra travel mug so we can take it downstairs to the studio."

"That sounds great. I think I froze my ass off shoveling the sidewalk and front doorway of your studio."

She shot a look at his delectable ass and shook her head. "Nope, your gorgeous ass is still intact." She grinned as she poured the coffee. "And that was very kind of you to shovel the walk. There's gotta be about a foot of snow out there."

"Yeah, and it's still coming down. Fun times for driving."

"Yeah. I hope your crew will be okay coming up here." She bit her lip as she shrugged into her jacket. "It sucks to fight snow on your day off."

He snorted as he grabbed both their travel mugs. "Are you kidding? They would probably treat it as an adventure. Most of the crew are pretty hardy. And I'm from Wyoming. We know snow."

Estelle locked the door behind them and headed down the stairs. She paused at the outer door at the ground floor, watching the snow fly past damn near horizontal. *Oh, this is going to be fun.* Taking a deep breath, she shoved the outer door open and braced her back against it long enough for Mark to step through. The wind buffeted the door at her back, making her feet skid on the icy sidewalk despite her thick boots.

Here goes. She let the door close and carefully moved over to her studio door. Mark thankfully stood behind her and blocked the wind. She appreciated his big body as she thrust her door open and stepped through. He followed with a big sigh.

"Yeah, okay, the wind might be a little more bitter here than in Wyoming."

She barked a laugh as she switched on the lights. "That's the effect from the Lake. Even Harbor Lake makes things wetter and colder."

"Good thing photoshoots are warm because of the lights."

"Thank the Goddess."

Not long after they turned on the lights, Amy, and Jayson and Kate Blackamber arrived. Estelle hadn't met Jayson's wife before, but something about the woman's demeanor set her at ease immediately. Her hazel gaze seemed filled with humor and wisdom, though she didn't appear much older than Estelle.

"Look who I found loitering out on the sidewalk." Amy pulled them inside and shut the door. "And Kate brought her famous goodies."

Kate laughed and the room sparkled. "Not so famous this time. I tried a new recipe for a sweet bread. Hopefully it turned out okay."

Jayson snorted and patted his flat belly. "I'm pretty sure it'll be great. Just make sure everyone grabs some before I eat it all."

Kate slapped his shoulder. "You have a whole one at home. Leave it for these hard-working people."

Jayson growled, literally growled, but he didn't appear to be too upset. Mark, however, stiffened at the growl and shifted closer to Estelle as she moved around the room, setting up lights while Amy made coffee in the kitchenette. He didn't get in the way, but he kept his body between Jayson and Estelle. *That's kinda weird.*

"Go be useful to Ms. Three-Hearts, will you?" Kate pointed at Estelle. "I'm going to make sure there's something to eat before all the huge, sexy firefighters get here."

"Yeah, yeah." Despite his grumpy words, Jayson smiled and winked at Estelle. "Do you want me to arrange the hay bales, Estelle?"

"Yes, please. I want them in front of the winter background today."

"I'll help, too."

Did Mark's voice sound tight? She shot him a look, but his back was to her as he followed Jayson into the corner with the hay bales. She frowned. There was something going on with him. She'd sensed it in the apartment, but even more so now that Jayson had arrived. *Like he's staking his claim.* She snorted softly to herself. *As if he needs to do that with Jayson. He's married.*

She was distracted when the door of her studio opened and someone stepped in. She turned to find a slightly balding man in a suit and heavy parka. He had a wool beanie over his head and his eyes widened when he found all the people in the room.

"Oh, excuse me. I didn't mean to interrupt."

Estelle frowned a little. "Mr. Duckworth? What are you doing here in this kind of weather?"

His smile turned warm as his gaze found her. "Ah, Ms. Three-Hearts. So nice to see you. I'm sorry to barge in like this, but it's come to my attention that one of my properties isn't quite up to code and I wanted to check over all the units to make sure this wasn't the one."

"Oh. Uh, okay. Will the inspection take long?" She shot a look at the clock. She had less than thirty minutes until the firefighters were supposed to arrive.

"Not too long. Why?"

"I have a photoshoot scheduled for today with the firefighters from Newberry for the charity calendar." She waved around the room to encompass the lights, backdrop, and Mark. "They don't have a lot of time off and I need to get this done in time to produce the calendar."

"Oh, of course, my dear. It won't take long at all. I'll

just get this unit done immediately and be on my way."

"Yeah, all right." Something felt off about this visit, but he seemed to be confident in what he was about as he headed to the back with the dressing rooms and water closet.

Before she could follow him, Amy pulled her phone away from her ear with a grimace. "The snow is messing with Hazel and the critters. She's not able to come with kittens and puppies today."

"Oh, all right." Estelle took a deep breath. "That's fine. We still have plenty of fire equipment and the Santa outfit. Uncle Jeff promised he'd be our hot Santa for the December shot."

Amy squealed with delight and clapped her hands. "Really? Oh my glory, Angelina and my Auntie Olga will be thrilled. They'll probably buy the calendar just for him."

"That's what I said." Estelle smiled, but her gaze slid back to the back rooms where Mr. Duckworth had gone.

She didn't like him poking around her studio, but she liked the idea of him poking around her apartment even less. Unfortunately, he was the owner of the building, and she didn't have a lot of say in the matter.

"I know this is going to be a success." Amy came up with the light meter. "Ready to test the shots?"

"Yeah." Estelle nodded sharply. "Ready."

****

Mark sensed Estelle's unease with Mr. Duckworth as the man headed for her back rooms, but he couldn't follow to keep an eye on him. He had his hands full with the hay bales and Jayson Blackamber. The man might be married, but Mark didn't know him well enough to know how domesticated he'd become with his wife. He thought werewolves mated for life, but he'd only heard of them connecting with other werewolves. Not with humans, and not with *Morukai.*

He'd never felt a woman's emotions as clearly as he felt Estelle's. *That's because I've never bonded with anyone.* He'd have to tell her, but he didn't want to do in front of all these strangers. Especially her assistant Amy. The young human woman was sweet enough, but she struck him as someone who couldn't keep a secret.

He and Jayson had just managed to get the hay bales into position when Mr. Duckworth returned to the main studio room.

"Everything looks fine here, Ms. Three-Hearts. You should be fine."

"Oh, good." Estelle didn't smile. "Will you be checking the upstairs units as well?"

Mr. Duckworth nodded. "It's part of knowing where a problem could be."

Estelle stiffened and unease wafted off her with the scent of rotting meat. "Right. Let me go up with you and let you into my apartment."

"That's not necessary. I can let myself in and check."

"Oh, no, I insist. I want to make sure my apartment is okay." *And I don't want you pawing through my stuff.* She didn't say the last aloud, but Mark could hear the subtext loud and clear. "Amy, can you make sure everything is set up? I won't be long."

She threw her coat over her shoulders and held the door for Mr. Duckworth before she followed him out into the snow. Mark didn't like the idea of her alone with Duckworth in her apartment, but he kept his ear tuned to the spaces above. He heard them tromp up the stairs and into the room overhead, but he lost them when the door to the studio opened and the other firefighters came in from the blowing snow.

"Hey, Mark. When did you get here?" Captain Knight beat the snow off his shoulders as he grasped Mark's forearm in a warm grip.

"I didn't leave Three Lakes yesterday. I figured it was wiser to stay in town. How was the drive up here?" Mark led him and the others to the kitchenette where Amy was handing out coffee with Kate.

"Lousy. We damn near slid off the road twice because of black ice under the snow." Knight shook his head. "It was smart of you to stay here. It'll be a trick to get back to Newberry later today." He looked around the studio. "Where's Estelle?"

Mark nodded his head toward the ceiling. "Upstairs with the building owner. Apparently, he needs to inspect his properties to be sure they're up to code."

Knight raised his salt-n-pepper eyebrows. "Did he have an inspector with him?"

"No, he came alone."

"And he didn't ask you to go with him?"

Mark shook his head. "I was in the middle of moving hay bales."

"Huh." Knight frowned and shot a look at the front door. "You said they went upstairs?"

"Yeah, but they should be back down here soon." Mark caught the sounds of footsteps on the steps to the second floor.

"Have some coffee, Captain. I'm sure Estelle will be right along." Amy handed him a tall paper cup of steaming coffee.

"Thanks." But Knight kept his gaze on the front door, a frown marring his brow.

Estelle pushed it open a few moments later and Mark strode over to her, sensing confusion and unease, but no fear.

"How did it go?" He took her coat from her.

"Fine. There's nothing wrong in my apartment." She shook her head. "I really didn't want him in there going through my things."

"Everything okay, Estelle?" Captain Knight gave her a

hug.

"Oh, Uncle Jeff. I'm glad you were able to make it with the rest of your crew." She squeezed him before stepping back, and Mark had to grit his teeth to keep from ripping her out of Knight's embrace.

"Yeah, it as a close thing with the roads the way they are."

"Oh no." She looked him over. "Everything okay?"

"Yeah, we're fine, but it's slick out there." He frowned and nodded to the door. "What's up with the building owner? Mark said something about the place being up to code?"

"Yeah." Estelle frowned as she picked up a piece of Kate's sweet bread. "Crichton Duckworth owns this building and a couple of others. He said someone had reported that one of his properties wasn't up to code, so he came to take a look." She frowned and chewed a few moments. "The strange thing is he's never done this before. Like ever. And anytime I have a maintenance issue, he always sends the property manager or a repair man. He never comes himself. This is the first time."

"Huh." Knight nodded, his own brows low. "Why were you upstairs with him?"

"Because I didn't want him going through my place without me. It seemed kinda creepily invasive."

"I can see that. But he said he didn't see anything wrong with your apartment?"

"Yeah, he said it looked okay."

"Huh." Knight rubbed his chin. "Tell you what. After our shoot, I'll go up and look the place over myself, if that'll make you feel better."

"Yeah, it would." Estelle smiled and some of her tension faded from her shoulders. "Thanks, Uncle Jeff."

"Not a problem. Shall we get this show on the road?" He shot a look at the other firefighters standing around drinking coffee and eating the sweet bread.

"Yes, sir." They all looked at Estelle and she set down her coffee.

"All right. We'll start with you." She pointed at the tallest member of the company and got to work.

Mark stood back and watched her set everything in motion like a small whirlwind. Between him and Jayson, the set pieces she wanted as background props came and went like the ebb and flow of the tides. Amy helped with lighting and costume arrangement to the amusement of the firefighters and Captain Knight. The younger woman didn't have a problem with helping the men show off a little more muscle.

Mark helped move some of the props and gave suggestions to make the arrangement of them look authentic, but otherwise, watched his woman work her creative magic. He was impressed, not only with her eye, but with her professionalism with the models in their various states of undress.

"She's amazing, isn't she?"

Mark focused on the person next to him with a start. Wise hazel eyes met his and a friendly smile curled Kate's lips as she rested her butt against the kitchenette counter. The woman wasn't particularly tall, but she seemed larger than life when standing next to him.

"Estelle? Yes. She really knows how to capture the models."

Kate nodded. "In more ways than one."

"What?" Mark shot her a startled look.

"Hi, I'm Kate Blackamber, local eccentric, Shaman to the Elder Races, and Speaker for the Goddess." Kate held out her hand, her expression expectant.

"Uh, hi." He clasped hers. "Mark Redfeather, Newberry firefighter."

"And?" When Mark didn't answer, she smiled. "Iris mentioned I should stop by to see how the shoot was going. There's quite a few of your crew who are part of the Elder

Races, but I've never encountered your type of energy. Which nation are you from?"

Oh, she means the First Peoples. "I'm from the Arapaho nation."

Kate nodded. "Is that where your people originated?"

He frowned. "My people?"

"Yeah, whichever Elder Race you belong to. Your energy is…" She tightened her lips. "Fiery."

Oh. He nodded and shot a look around to make sure the humans in the room couldn't overhear them.

"I'm a Firebird." He'd never said those words out loud together and unease trickled through him at the reminder of his otherness with regard to Estelle.

Kate tilted her head. "That's a new one for me. I'm not familiar with that Elder Race. Are your people rare?"

He nodded. "I'm related to the Thunderbirds of legend. One in every two million Thunderbirds is a Firebird. I was the lucky one."

She rubbed her chin. "You don't sound all that thrilled."

He shrugged, pushing away the old pain. "It's said the Firebird is a harbinger of cataclysm and world change. When my parents realized my heritage, they didn't want what they got."

"I'm so sorry they saw you that way." She shook her head. "The things people do to their kids all in the name of old beliefs and fears. Did everyone in your family feel that way?"

He shrugged. "Not my grandmother or my twin, though we've drifted apart."

She raised her eyebrows. "Is your twin a Firebird too?"

"No, he's a Thunderbird like the rest." Many times throughout their childhood, Mark had been envious of his brother and the easy connection with the rest of their family. But he'd grown to accept his place in the world, and what he needed to do to protect others. "The irony?

Thomas is also a firefighter. A Hotshot, the crazy ground crews that try to stop the fires from spreading."

Kate laughed. "Two halves of the same apple."

Mark froze, the cadence if the words echoing in his memory. "My grandmother used to say that."

"She was a wise woman." Kate smiled and turned her gaze to where Estelle asked one of firefighters to raise an ax against his bare shoulder. "Have you told her what you are?"

Mark's gut sank and his shoulders slumped. "No. I don't know how." He scanned the room to be sure no one was listening, though he suspected her werewolf husband could hear just fine. "We mated last night and I accidentally bonded to her."

Kate raised her eyebrows and he shook his head. "She doesn't know about it or what it means. But she's human, and I'm...not."

Kate took a deep breath in, letting it out slow. "Yeah, that's a tough one."

She watched the unfolding photoshoot for a few moments, and Mark's concerns bloomed. *Aw hell, if the Morukai is stumped, I'm so screwed.*

"You're going to have to tell her." Kate nodded sharply as if someone had given her a directive. She turned her gaze on him and he swore he saw stars in her eyes. "She needs to know and she's not your typical human. And if you trust her, you'll reap rewards you haven't even thought of yet. I know it's a lot to trust a human with these kinds of secrets, but you might be surprised with how many of the humans here know about the Elder Races. You're better off here with her than anywhere else. And she has her own secrets."

Mark raised his chin. "How do you know that?"

She gave him an enigmatic smile that morphed into a grin. "I pay attention." She winked before she sobered. "You do need to tell her, Mark. She has a right to know so she can make her own decisions."

"And if she runs from me? I'm stuck with someone who fears me too much to love me."

Kate nodded. "That's the price of honesty, isn't it? She's stronger than you think, and honesty between partners is huge. You don't want to lose her? Then tell her and trust her with your secrets. Otherwise, it's just a matter of time before she leaves."

Mark's stomach sank as if loaded down with too much frybread. Estelle couldn't leave. He needed her in ways he hadn't even considered. The Firebird screeched in protest and warning, and he swallowed hard. He must have known what he was doing when he marked her, but humans were predictable in their unpredictability. *I could lose her.*

The Firebird screamed again. *Our mate. Ours!*

He nodded. "Yeah, I know."

"It'll work out, Mark." Kate clapped him on the shoulder. "Trust your gut, your Firebird. He knows more than you think he does."

He snorted. "You really think so?"

She laughed, her eyes sparkling like stars again. "I know so, *hookesiteeno*."

The nickname for *Little Fire* his grandmother had called him brought tears to his eyes and his throat closed. He couldn't do anything other than nod and give her a watery smile. She patted his shoulder and left him to head over to her husband, looking for all the world like an ordinary human woman. *She's so much more than that.* He'd heard the *Morukai* were not only the speakers for the Goddess, but sometimes an embodiment of Her. He had no doubt Kate Blackamber filled both roles well.

The question was, could he trust himself as much as he trusted her?

CHAPTER NINE

Estelle kept an eye on Kate Blackamber while she talked to Mark. Estelle's shoulders tightened and jealousy made an unusual appearance. *Why the hell am I jealous of Kate talking to Mark? He's not my boyfriend and she's married.* But the way he listened to Kate as if she was offering the secrets of the universe made Estelle uneasy. And when Mark appeared to get choked up, Estelle had to tamp down on the urge to rush to his defense.

What the hell is wrong with me?

She took a moment to rub her eyes with one hand before she fired off the last few shots of the current firefighter model.

"All right, that's great. Thanks." She didn't even remember the guy's name or if she'd managed to capture any decent shots of him. "Let's take a short break while we upload these images to the computer. I could use some more coffee."

She set her camera aside after she removed the SD card. She tightened her hand around it as Kate laughed and clapped her hand on Mark's shoulder. *I won't get upset. He's not mine.* She had no idea where the possessiveness came from. She normally needed much more time with someone to have such feelings.

"Do you want to do the gear and truck background next, Estelle?" Amy paused in the kitchenette as Estelle served herself some black gold.

"Yeah, that'll be good."

She ran her hand over her neck as she tried to calm down. *Breathe, breathe.* She'd never reacted this way over a guy, especially a guy she'd just met. But something fired her blood each time another woman got near him. *Maybe my period is starting early.* Normally her cycle was fairly regular, but how else could she explain her easy temper?

Maybe it was stress over Mr. Duckworth's visit. Something about it had her hackles up. She hadn't wanted him in her apartment alone, but she'd never felt like that before. He'd been polite and professional, but her gut told her something was off. She knew he'd been trying to raise the rent on both his professional tenants as well as the residential ones, but the market hadn't supported that move, and he'd backed off.

"May I take a look at the raw images?" Kate Blackamber appeared at her shoulder as her husband and Mark rearranged the studio.

"What?"

"The images of these hot men and women. You have to upload them off the card, right?" Kate pointed at the computer.

"Oh, yes. Right. Sorry, I was off in la-la land. You want to see them?" Estelle frowned.

"Yes, may I?" Kate nodded.

"Uh, yeah, okay. I guess." She returned to her desk and opened the laptop, shoving the SD card into the slot. "They won't look as good as the final product and most of them are going to be duds."

"Really?" Kate raised her eyebrows. "But you're such a good photographer."

"I am," she agreed with a nod. "But even I need to take

about two hundred photos to get maybe two good ones. Sometimes the ratio is even smaller. Digital cameras really make it easier for us now. We used to go through film like it was water."

"Wow." Kate sounded impressed. "That's crazy."

Estelle nodded as she uploaded the images. She'd already taken close to three hundred just on the two firefighters she'd seen that morning. Some she could tell would be tossed immediately. Blurred motion or slightly out of focus shots caught her eye immediately. But there were a few that made her heart flutter with their perfection.

"Sweet glory, those are beautiful." Kate's exclamation warmed Estelle's heart. "You have an amazing eye. Look at how you captured the shadows on his chest and arms. That's so striking."

"This one?" Estelle clicked on the thumbnail image and enlarged it.

"Yeah." Kate shook her head. "That's fantastic. I'm definitely getting one of these calendars."

"Oh, yeah? That good?" Jayson sounded skeptical as he wandered to them to peer over her shoulder. "Holy shit! Those are amazing."

"I told you." Kate thumped him in the arm. "She's an expert photographer. She captures magic."

"Thanks, but they'll look even better once I've used Photoshop to clean them up."

"Damn, Torrington, she made you actually look handsome." One of the firefighters teased another and Estelle realized she had a crowd behind the computer.

"Shut up, Mayfair. It's gonna take extra magic to prettify your ugly mug."

Estelle listened to the ribbing with half an ear as the others wandered away. She tried to get her mind back on what she needed to be doing, but once the card was empty, she'd have to focus on the photography. *And ignoring the women around Mark.*

"He's not interested in anyone but you, you know." Kate's voice surprised her with both its softness and its conviction.

"Who?"

"Mark Redfeather, the hot Arapaho firefighter helping my sexy husband move things around the room." Kate nodded toward the men.

"How would you know that?" Estelle tried to keep her voice light, but her mouth tightened over her teeth.

"Because he hasn't taken his eyes off you the whole time you were shooting the others. I'm pretty sure he's smitten."

Estelle snorted and shook her head. "We've known each other a handful of days."

"Sometimes that's all it takes. It was the same way with me and Jayson. Of course, he was sure of us the moment he spoke to me." She rolled her eyes and shook her head. "It took me a little while longer to realize what he knew all along. Damn, overconfident former Navy SEAL."

Estelle choked as her gaze found Jayson laughing with Mark. "He was a Navy SEAL?"

"Yeah. Fast, smart, lethal, and sexy. I was totally won over."

Estelle snorted with amusement. "Yeah, that sounds like a helluva combination."

"It was for me." She turned her head back to Estelle. "Mark's a little like that. He runs toward danger rather than away from it. He's fast, smart, and sexy."

"You think he's sexy?" Unease skittered through her as she pulled the SD card out of the computer slot.

"Yeah, in a general way. That's why we buy these calendars, right?" Kate nodded to her husband. "That's why I have Jayson. He's the real deal after enjoying the fantasy." She returned her gaze to Estelle's. "More than likely Mark's unsure how you'll feel about him after spending all this time with these other sexy men. It's amazing how guys get nervous about pictures in a calendar."

"You think he's worried I'm interested in someone else?"

Kate shrugged. "I think he wants you to know the real him and hopes that it'll be enough to keep your attention while you're looking through the lens at all the hot male bodies."

Estelle blinked. "He thinks I'm interested in all the pretty men who come through here?"

Kate shook her head. "I don't know what he thinks, but I know he wants to show you his true nature, and he's worried about what you'll think of it. Talk to him. I know he cares a lot more about you than he's letting on."

"Now?"

"When you're done today. You have a few more firefighters to photograph, right?" Kate waved at the men standing in the kitchenette.

Estelle sighed. "Yup. We better get back to it." She rose, plugging the SD card into the camera's slot. "All right. Let's get the next batch of images. I want this one to be a group shot. Mark, do you want to join them?"

To her relief, a wide smile graced his lips. "Sure. I managed to get my gear out of my truck this morning so it's not half frozen."

"Great. Change into your gear and we'll be ready to go."

The hot men in turnout gear settled themselves on the hay bales in front of the truck background, and Amy handed them additional props of the American flag, a bunting, and little sticks that they'd later Photoshop to look like sparklers.

Mark had disappeared into the bathroom, but came out later with his turnout pants and suspenders wearing his helmet. Estelle shivered at his masculine beauty and her pussy flexed with the memory of his diligent attention.

Damn, they're all sexy, but he's the sexiest. She took a moment to wipe the drool from the corner of her mouth and got to work.

Fortunately, all the firefighters, including her uncle, were patient with her tweaking and positioning of their bodies, limbs, and props, and she got many mouth-watering images from them. Her concerns about Mark's interest in Kate melted into the background, and she was able to enjoy herself.

Once she got the sultry images, she let them fool around so she could capture some candid and goofy shots. She loved watching the big, muscular, heroic men grin and tease each other, and even caught her uncle laughing hard enough to cry.

But the real tears of mirth started when she told her uncle he'd be the last image in the calendar as the sexy, hot, silver-fox Santa.

"What? No, I didn't think you were serious."

"Oh, hell yeah, I was serious. We'll probably sell the majority of calendars just for that image." She rested her camera against her shoulder, all her weight on one leg. "Don't worry, I'll make it look tasteful. Just get your Don Juan on, and we'll do this."

"My 'Don Juan'?" Jeff raised his eyebrows. "You've got to be kidding me."

"Come on, Captain. It's for a good cause. The women love this stuff."

"The women love the young guys, not someone who's older than dirt." Jeff shook his head.

"You're not older than dirt, and lots of women love to see the older men strut their stuff." Amy smiled with happy appeal. "Come on, I'll help you. We even have the suit coat and hat, and a bag full of presents already wrapped."

"Seriously?"

Mark grinned and held up a few of the ones he and Jayson were shoving into a red sack. Estelle took a moment to enjoy the way his muscles flexed without a shirt covering them. *Glory be, he's very sexy.* Too bad he had to drive back to Newberry tonight. She ignored the disappointment of sleeping alone.

"It'll be great, Captain. We'll be able to say with confidence that our captain has experience and grit." Mark laughed as the captain scowled.

"Please, Uncle Jeff?" Estelle turned on her wheedling voice. "It's for a good cause and everyone's doing their part."

He sighed and shook his head as he ran his hands over his suspenders as if to loosen them. "All right."

"Great." She nodded sharply. "Now lose the shirt and shrug into the coat."

"What? I have to take off my shirt?"

"Well, yeah. All the other guys did." Amy nodded, holding up the Santa coat.

"But they're at least fifteen years younger than me."

Estelle opened her mouth to tell him it didn't matter, but the words stuck in her throat as she caught Mark mumbling, "Not really." She turned to ask him what he meant, but he'd joined the other firefighters in ribbing her uncle about taking off his shirt.

"Hey, now, if he's concerned he can't live up to your standards, that's all right." Estelle shrugged as she got ready to snap some images.

"Who said I was concerned?"

Estelle hid her smile as Jeff shrugged his suspenders off his shoulders and pulled his shirt over his head. He threw the shirt at Torrington and strutted over to the hay bales with his chest out and his shoulders back. She shot Amy a wink, but kept her expression smooth when she looked at her uncle.

Despite his worry, Jeff had kept his body in decent condition as he approached sixty years. He had salt-and-pepper hair on his chest and belly, but while he'd gone softer than the younger men, he still had his six pack and ridged pectorals. She didn't think the older women who bought the calendar would be disappointed. *Or the older gay men, either.*

"Great. Now stand in front of the truck with your feet shoulder-width apart, dip your chin a little. Amy, can you adjust the hat to a rakish angle? Thanks." Estelle looked through her camera. "Yeah, great. Now grab your suspenders and pull them off your chest just a little. That's it."

She had Amy pull one suspender off his shoulder along with the Santa coat and look coyly out from under the hat. Next she had him sit on the hay bales with his feet crossed at the ankle as if kickin' back after a hard night delivering gifts. Soon the other men were making suggestions, some sexy, some fun, and she kept snapping pictures to download later.

At last they broke for lunch and she uploaded the images to her computer, the men teasing each other with good-natured digs. Kate and Jayson helped with doling out the food, and Kate managed to produce more cookies and goodies to share. With the holiday decorations, the Santa outfit, and the snow, the whole day took on a festive feeling as if they'd all taken a holiday vacation. Estelle had to admit she enjoyed having her studio full of hot men.

Especially one in particular.

But it was more than that. With her brother's reconstructive surgeries, the holidays were often lonely, especially for her birthday on New Year's Day. Having these men here, eating, laughing, teasing each other with her uncle. It felt like family.

Emotion welled up and damn near spilled out her eyes. *Family.* The word felt alien, a lost concept in her life. Most of the time it didn't bother her to be alone, but the holidays, particularly around her birthday, were harder than the rest of the year.

"Hey, are you okay?"

She gasped and blinked hard, Mark's voice intruding on her thoughts. She turned to him and tried to smile, but it came across a little wobbly because he frowned.

"What's wrong, Estelle?" He searched her eyes as he stood in her space. Concern and intensity wafted off of him like a new cologne.

"Nothing. Nothing's wrong." She shook her head before she waved toward the others in the kitchenette. "You're a family. I can see it. You have your petty squabbles and your teasing, but you're family. It's been a long time for me."

"A long time?"

"Since I've had family around at the holidays."

"Oh, Estelle." He gathered her into his arms so fast she didn't have time to worry about who saw them. "I'm very sorry to hear that. Let's change that this year, yeah?"

"It's fine. You don't have to do anything." She straightened and pulled out of his arms. "I'll be fine."

"Hey, it's not fine. This year, let's spend the holidays together, you and me."

"Just you and me?" She raised an eyebrow and shot a look toward the other firefighters in the kitchenette.

"Just you and me, or you, me, and the fire crew if I have to work that night." He shrugged as he captured her gaze again. "But not just you this year. Okay?"

She searched his eyes. "Are you sure? We just met and I don't want to overstep or become clingy."

He smiled, warmth lighting his gaze. "I don't think you're the kind of woman who becomes clingy. You strike me as too independent for that."

"Hoh!" She barked the word as she wiped away the suspicious moisture. "You haven't seen me at the holidays yet." She grimaced. "But if you'd like me to spend them with you, I'd be happy to take you up on that."

"Deal." He leaned forward as if to kiss her, but seemed

to remember that the rest of his crew stood in the room, and pulled back.

She understood his reluctance to get more ribbing from his crew, but she wished he'd kissed her nonetheless.

"The images are loaded, Estelle." Amy's voice intruded on her fantasies and Estelle blinked, nodding.

"Okay. Let me take a look at them and I'll let you know if you are free to head home." Her stomach clenched at the idea of Mark leaving, but she didn't have any claim on him, and he had to work for a living.

"I hope mine are good. I don't think I'll ever live down the Silver Fox Santa gig." Uncle Jeff shook his head. He'd donned his shirt again and removed his turnout gear. "It's embarrassing."

"Not if they look good, Captain." Amy shot him a cheeky grin. "If they look really hot, we'll sell so many calendars, every building in Three Lakes will get smoke and carbon monoxide detectors. Heck, we might even sell enough to get detectors in every town from here to Newberry."

"That would be a great thing. I want every house, business, school, and municipal building with an early warning system." Estelle nodded as she opened up the file folder with the images.

Remarkable beauty met her gaze as she clicked on image after image. Not all of them were good enough for the calendar, but there were several she'd have to consider. Her eyes blurred with tears again. They looked so beautiful for such a great cause, and their generosity warmed her heart. *Get it together. They're gonna think you're on your period or something.*

She made sure to look over the images of her uncle as Santa and there were at least two pictures she could use in the calendar. The best one had him smirking at the camera when someone said something funny and he'd hammed it up.

"Yep, you look good, Uncle Jeff. No need to take your shirt off again unless you want to." She winked at him and laughed as he rolled his eyes.

"Yeah, yeah. Not gonna happen. The only silver you're gonna see this holiday season will be the utensils on the table."

She laughed. "Promises, promises."

She shook her head, but caught Mark's movement out of the corner of her eye as he leaned in to whisper something to Jeff. She wanted to watch them with both eyes, but she had to make sure all the images were downloaded successfully. She didn't want them to be screwed up before she had a chance to really look them over.

"Hey, Estelle, do you have plans for Christmas? You're not staying here in Three Lakes alone, are you?"

Jeff's question caught her by surprise, especially when the entire studio silenced. She turned her head and found everyone's eyes on her. *What's the big deal?* They all seemed to be holding their breaths like the firefighters in that old 80's movie about the fire captain with the extra-long nose.

"Uh, well, I hadn't really thought about it yet."

"You haven't thought about it? Christmas is in a week. Hell, even the Solstice is in two days." Jeff shook his head. "Why don't you come down to Newberry to share the holiday with us?"

"Yeah, you should come." The rest of the firefighters nodded and agreed.

"I don't know…"

"You can stay in the extra room in the fire station and we cook a mean feast. It'll be great." Jeff gave her a hopeful grin. "What do you say?"

"Well, I promised to spend it with Mark."

"Excellent." Jeff grinned. "I'll make sure to schedule him to work that night so you come to Newberry."

"Uncle Jeff."

He spread his hands with a wide-eyed look. "What?"

"All right, I'll come to Newberry for Christmas and you all can cook for me. No promises on the dishes though."

While the guys groaned, she let the idea of spending the holidays with the fire family settle into her heart. Maybe it would be just what she needed. And if Mark had to work that night, at least she'd spend what time he wasn't dealing with fires to celebrate. *Maybe this year will be full of more cheer than usual.* She could only hope.

CHAPTER TEN

The time between the photoshoot and the Christmas holiday slipped through Estelle's fingers like sand in a sieve. She managed to pick the images for the calendar, enhance them, and get them to the printer to make the mock-up sample. She also coordinated with Hazel and the Newberry FD for newspaper articles and outreach. The calendar would go on sale just after the Christmas holiday, and be a New Year's special. From the images she'd taken, it was going to be a hit, especially her Silver Fox Santa at the end.

Mark had texted and called her several times in the intervening days, but they'd both been busy. Apparently, the locals thought the snow and cold would help keep the fire danger to a minimum despite their choices to leave candles burning, engage in unsafe wiring of lights, and overloading outlets. Mark had been working enough to sound exhausted when she called him.

Her own schedule made for long days. She worked on the calendar images in between holiday family portraits, some complete with pets. She'd always found that entertaining, but could understand the appeal. Most of her favorite shots of the firefighters were with the critters from the SPCA.

By the time Christmas Eve rolled around, they had almost six thousand dollars' worth of pre-orders on the calendar, and it appeared the SDEB program would be a success. She'd noticed her own apartment had been missing smoke alarms when she moved in, and she'd bought two from the local hardware store just in case she set something on fire. *Why the hell wouldn't Mr. Duckworth have alarms in his building?* It was a good thing she'd put in for this program. Then all the residents in the building would be safer.

Estelle had just finished packing her overnight bag when her phone rang. She picked it up and found Mark's name on her screen.

"Hey, Mark. What's up?"

"I was just checking to see if you were on your way." His voice held excitement. "Are you?"

"Not quite yet. I just finished packing and I need to get a couple of things from my studio, but then I'll be on my way." She shot a look out the window. It was dark and cloudy, but hadn't snowed in a day or two. "The roads should be pretty clear. Are you sure I can't bring anything for the feasts? I know how much you guys can eat."

"Nope. We got it covered. Just bring yourself. I'm looking forward to seeing you."

His voice deepened and hot arousal shot through her. Damn, the man lit her on fire in all the best ways.

"Me too." She grinned as she headed for the door. "Give me about ten to fifteen minutes, and I'll be on my way."

"Okay. Hey, Estelle?" An odd note crept into his voice.

"Yeah?" She paused as she shrugged into her coat.

"When you get here, I have something I need to talk to you about."

She bit her bottom lip and frowned. "All right. Is

everything okay?"

"Yeah, yeah, it's fine. I just have something important to discuss."

"A good something-important or a serious something-important?" What if he'd grown tired of her already? They hadn't known each other long. Was he having second-thoughts?

"Both, but more on the good side."

She paused at her door beside her bag. "Do you want me to stay here rather than come down to Newberry? I don't want things to be awkward for the holidays."

"No, shit. Definitely no. I really want to see you, hold you, and uh, more, but I also don't want to spring anything on you, okay?"

"Yeah, okay. You're sure?"

"I'm sure. Call me when you're on the road?"

"Yeah, I will." She bit her lip again. "Are you really sure? Because I can stay here."

"Please come to Newberry, Estelle. I really want to see you."

"Okay. I'll call you when I'm on the way."

"Okay. Drive safely, please." His voice had warmed again and she took some solace from it.

"I will. See you soon."

They ended the call and she took a moment to gather her emotions and wits. He sounded like he wanted her to be there, and she'd been looking forward to it despite her exhaustion. What could he want to talk to her about? He didn't give the impression he wanted to break up, not that they'd talked about being exclusive, but it sounded more serious than excitement over a Christmas gift he'd found. What could it be?

"You're not gonna find out if you don't get going."

She mentally slapped herself and grabbed her bag as she took one last look around. She hadn't left any lights on or candles burning. She hadn't left the appliances on, and she'd made sure to close her chimney flue. Everything was set for her to leave.

She grabbed her bag and locked her apartment door, the last one to leave the building. Pretty much all her neighbors were off with family this year. The building had been quiet for the last couple of days, a rare event with four apartments and two businesses in it. She hadn't had the chance to enjoy it as she'd been working so much on her projects. But the silence filled the hallway and she let it seep into her as she made her way to the ground floor.

Outside, the evening was cold but still. No snow or wind yet, but she suspected it wouldn't last long. She lugged her bag out to her jeep and pressed the automatic start button to let it warm before she returned to her studio. She wanted to make sure she brought her good camera and the sample of the calendar for the firefighters to see before it came out to be sold.

She unlocked the door and pushed inside, grateful for the break in the cold. She flipped on the lights and headed for her desk. The laptop clicked on with a brush of her fingers and she settled into the chair to verify she'd answered all her emails. She slowly thawed as she clicked through the programs, making sure everything was in order.

She was so focused on finishing up she didn't smell the smoke until her store-bought smoke alarm screamed from the wall beside the bathroom. Estelle jerked to her feet, sending her chair careening across the studio as the white smoke billowed from the ceiling. Panic welled up in her throat and cut off her breath as she stood rooted to the floor while the smoke alarm blared. *Oh shit. WhatdoIdo? WhatdoIdo?* Her mind went blank for a few precious seconds and her heart hammered in her chest.

Move, you idiot!

She jolted into motion, grabbing the computer and shutting it down as she yanked the power cord out of it. She shoved it onto a carrying case and added the calendar mock up with it. She started to cough as the fire caught the beams above her head. *Damn, that was fast.*

Estelle glanced upwards to watch the flames skitter across the ceiling as if feeding on something more than dry wood and plaster. Had someone doused the ceiling with accelerant? It took her a few moments to realize it wasn't the ceiling, but the floor of the apartment above. Her apartment. Had she accidentally left something burning? *It's not possible. I checked.*

It didn't matter now. The walls of her studio sprouted flames and she realized she'd waited too long to get out. She was trapped in an empty burning building, and no one would know until it was too late.

Sweet glory, it's happening again.

She shook her head. *Call the fire department and get down.*

Estelle flattened herself to the floor beneath her desk and grabbed her phone. The air had grown hot and thick with smoke, making her throat burn. Her eyes teared, blurring the numbers, but she managed to find 911 on the digital keypad.

"Nine-one-one, what's your emergency?"

"Oh, glory, please help. There's a fire in the brick building along Harbor Lake Road."

"Ma'am, what's your address?"

She rattled off the building number, coughing and crying.

"Ma'am, are you in a safe place?"

"No. I'm trapped inside. I can't get out. There are flames everywhere. Please, send help."

"I'm contacting the Newberry fire department now, along with Sheriff Boulderson. Stay low to the floor and cover your mouth and nose if possible. Is there another exit to your location?"

She shook her head before she realized the 9-1-1 operator couldn't see it. "No, it's blocked with more flames."

"Hold on, I've alerted the fire department and the sheriff. They should be there soon. I'll stay on the line with you. Are you close to the floor, ma'am?"

"Yes."

"Give me your name, ma'am."

"Estelle Three-Hearts." The room started to swim in her vision and her lungs struggled to find clean air. "Oh, glory, it's so hot in here and I can't breathe."

"Hold on, Ms. Three-Hearts. Help is on the way. Where in the building are you located?"

"Ground floor in the Three Hearts Photography studio."

"Keep your eyes on the front door. Help is on the way."

She rolled toward the doors, her gaze searching for the pewter sky through the flames, but tears blurred everything into a flickering black and orange swirl. *I'm so sorry, Mark. I should've just gotten in the car and gone.* It was too late now. She couldn't get out, couldn't breathe. She'd die here of asphyxiation and burns. *Oh Goddess, tell Mark I wanted more time with him. Tell him I loved being with him.*

The crackling of the flames grew louder until it sounded as if her kettle screamed in heated protest. *Maybe it's the smoke detector still going off.* But the sound grew in volume and she opened her eyes to look around. The glass in the front of her building shattered and the flames leapt for freedom. *I should try to get out.* But she'd lost the ability to move. *Too hard to breathe.*

Black edged the corners of her vision just as something large and winged landed on the street outside. It looked like a huge bird in the shape of an eagle, but much bigger, and completely made of flames. A tall flaming crest rose from the back of its head and a long burning tail stood straight out behind it. Blue glowing eyes met hers and the creature screamed, launching itself into the air again. Great talons scraped the pavement, leaving smoking furrows, and she realized what had arrived.

Sweet Goddess, it's a firebird.

She wanted to look more, but her head swam and she couldn't breathe. She tried to hold onto consciousness, but it slipped away into the hot, velvet dark.

****

Mark screamed as his mate dropped her head to the floor, succumbing to the smoke and heat. For a moment, he panicked. He could fly into the burning building in his natural form, but he couldn't touch her. The only way would be to shift into his human disguise, but while he wouldn't get badly burned, it didn't have the same imperviousness to flame as his natural form.

Fuck it.

Mark concentrated, focusing on the fire. It called to him, but he turned his attention to changing its direction. *Up*, he urged with his wings. *Go higher into the upper floors. You'll find more fuel there.*

At first, the fire ignored him, crackling and growling on the first floor, but eventually his offering of more fuel attracted the flames and they retreated from the studio. Mark dropped to the ground and shifted into his human disguise. He didn't have much time to get Estelle out before the fire returned.

He ran through the broken windows, searching for where he'd last seen her. Everything looked different from when he'd been here for the photoshoot and he couldn't get a sense of the space. But he found one pale hand curled into a fist on the floor under the desk and he skidded to a halt beside her.

Oh, Goddess of Fire, protect my mate. His heart contracted in fear, but he shoved it aside as he dragged her out from under the desk to the floor. He didn't waste time checking for a pulse. The fire wouldn't remain distracted very long and he needed her to be safe before he dealt with it.

He rolled her onto her back, noting she had her camera wrapped around her neck. Is that what she came in for? He pulled it off and set it beside the carrying case for her laptop. *She must have tried to save those two items when she realized the room was on fire.* Dropping to one knee, he grabbed her pant leg with his left hand and rolled over her body, pulling it up onto his shoulders as he came to his feet. She draped around him like a sweet-scented shawl, her head resting against his right shoulder.

"Hold on for me, Estelle." She didn't stir at his whisper as he bent down and grasped her camera and the laptop case. "Let's get you out of here."

He shot a look at the ceiling as he headed for the front of the studio. The fire wanted to return to the ground floor, to consume everything within reach, and it was done waiting. He shifted into a trot to get out just before the flames roared back into the studio. He made it to the street outside as the room filled with fire.

Thank you, Goddess.

He gently set Estelle down against the retaining wall across the road toward Harbor Lake, and checked her vitals. While she might have suffered some smoke inhalation and minor first degree burns on her hands, her pulse remained steady. He rested his head against hers for a few moments, grateful he'd gotten to Three Lakes in time. He'd never flown so fast in his life, and he suspected Captain Knight would be furious with him for not being with the crew.

A loud crash sounded and he turned to watch the fire consume the building, the upper floors collapsing into the ground floor. Sorrow shifted through him. Estelle had lost everything, her home, her studio, all the photography equipment. And she wasn't making any money from the sales of the calendars. That would all go to the SDEB program. He wanted to help put out the fire, but he had none of his turnout gear, and the majority of the crew didn't know he wasn't human.

Estelle doesn't know, either.

That's what he'd wanted to tell her when she arrived in Newberry. He needed to tell her about his Firebird, that he had mated with her for life. He had to explain that no matter what, he was bound to her, even if she didn't want to be with him. He'd always look out for her, protect her, know where she was in the world simply because of their bond.

It wasn't long before the sheriff of Three Lakes arrived. He and a bunch of volunteers started a bucket line to keep the fire from spreading to neighboring buildings and vehicles, but Estelle's building was a total loss. The sheriff, a huge giant of a man, spied them across the road and came their way, his sharp eyes taking in their appearance.

"Hey folks. Are you all right?"

"Yes, sir. My name's Mark Redfeather, and I'm a firefighter with the Newberry Fire Department. I pulled Ms. Three-Hearts out of the building before it was engulfed."

The sheriff eyed him a few moments before he dropped to a crouch beside Estelle. Even folded in half, his head came up to Mark's chest.

"You got her out, but don't have your gear?" The sheriff looked around. "Where's the rest of your crew?"

"I, uh, got here first, but I didn't have my gear with me."

To be honest, he didn't need it, but he hadn't had time to waste when the FD got the call about Estelle. The sheriff stared at him a little longer, eyes narrowed. He seemed to be taking in more details than Mark could see, but he kept his stone-like silence a few seconds more.

SIOBHAN MUIR

"All right, Mr. Redfeather." The sheriff got to his feet and held Mark's gaze. "Are you Elder Races, sir?"

The question damn near knocked the wind out of Mark, but he shot a look over his shoulder before he nodded. "Yes, Sheriff."

"Ah, okay. That makes sense, then. Kate mentioned she'd met someone new from the Newberry Fire Department. Must be you." He held out his hand. "Sheriff Bruce Boulderson. Glad you got here when you did. I don't think Ms. Three-Hearts would've made it."

He nodded to the road as flashing lights arrived behind the bucket line. "You got a story to tell your crew?"

Mark followed his gaze and sighed. "No, sir, but I couldn't let Ms. Three-Hearts burn to death." He hesitated before he met Boulderson's gaze. "She's my mate."

"Hoo-boy, no wonder you got here so damn quick. You know she's human, right?"

Mark nodded.

"Does she know about you?"

He shook his head.

"Hoo-boy, that's gonna be a tough one." Boulderson rubbed the back of his neck. "Let the paramedics take a look at her while we figure out a decent reason for you to be here without your crew, or a coat. Maybe Kate knows a way to let Estelle in on the secret."

The big sheriff waved the paramedics over as Mark knelt to check on Estelle again. She seemed all right, but she didn't open her eyes or wake. He scrambled out of the way as the paramedics leapt out and got her bundled onto a gurney. They asked him a few questions and he answered as best he could, but he had to leave her to their capable ministrations.

When the rest of the Newberry FD arrived, Boulderson made up a story about Mark being in town visiting Kate Blackamber, which was why he'd gotten to the fire first. Captain Knight wasn't thrilled with his absence, but he

106

accepted the sheriff's explanation without too much comment. Because he didn't have his gear, Mark kept out of the way while the rest of the crew contained the blaze, but he kept looking toward the ambulance. He hoped Estelle didn't have too much damage and he'd have a chance to talk to her about their connection.

Or rather his connection to her.

He'd never met a family member who'd bonded to a human, and didn't know how he'd reveal the secret to her. The Elder Races tended to hide their otherness from the humans, finding it wiser to keep their distance than reveal their true natures. But he'd bonded with Estelle before he could stop himself, and now he couldn't keep the secret from her.

He watched as the ambulance closed its doors and headed toward the Three Lakes Medical Clinic, wishing he could go with her. But he was already in enough trouble with the captain. He stayed until the blaze was contained and everything was checked and re-checked. The captain gave him the hairy eyeball a few times, but no one said anything out of line.

Mark was less worried about the captain than he was about Estelle. And he wasn't sure she'd think him anything but crazy when she did find out his secret.

Or frightening.

That thought didn't make him feel better.

CHAPTER ELEVEN

Estelle left her eyes closed after the nurse finished with her and rested, but her mind kept whirling like a kid on a merry-go-round. Snippets of memory filtered through the morass of swirling thought. The firebird on the pavement outside her burning studio. Mark's voice and presence beside her against the retaining wall. The sheriff and Mark talking about the Elder Races, and the sheriff asking if she knew about Mark.

Know what about him?

She hadn't heard his response, but from the sheriff's reaction, it hadn't been positive. She'd kept her eyes closed through the paramedics moving her and the ride to the hospital. Mark hadn't come with her, but she pretended to be asleep while they checked her over. She didn't feel like talking or responding to questions at the moment. She simply wanted to think and sort out what she'd heard and seen.

Had she really seen a firebird? She'd been close to blacking out when the huge flaming avian landed on the street outside, but her gut swore it had been real. It had looked exactly like the firebird in her dream from the time of the fire in her childhood home. The creature's blue glowing eyes had stared at her as if they'd understood who she was and what she needed. *Just like in my dream from before.*

But then Mark was there and he'd pulled her out of the building. *How did he get there so fast? I thought he was in Newberry.*

She must have been out longer than she thought. But the conversation with the sheriff while she pretended to be unconscious made her wonder. What the hell were the Elder Races and what didn't she know about Mark?

As if conjured by her thoughts, someone stepped into her corner of the clinic and paused by the bed. The smoky scent she remembered from making love with Mark filtered in along with the oxygen from the tube in her nose. His warm hand wrapped around hers as he settled into the chair beside her. He rested his elbows on the bed, but said nothing, and the waiting got too much for her. She opened her eyes and took in his face.

He looked tired and soot streaked as if he'd been in the fire himself. *Of course, he was. He dragged my ass out.* But sorrow striped his dark brown irises along with the exhaustion. She recalled their conversation before she left her apartment and swallowed hard. *Oh glory, he really does have something serious to tell me.* Did everyone else know? The sheriff seemed to understand the secret. Was he going to tell her he was married?

"Hey there, *beebeenei*. How are you feeling?"

She tried to speak, but her voice came out in a raspy croak. She shook her head and pointed to the pitcher of water beside the bed. "Please?"

He scrambled to pour her some and made sure to hold it steady for her to drink, his expression worried. When she'd finished, he took the cup away as she cleared her throat enough to speak.

"How long have I been here?"

He shot a look at his phone. "A couple of hours, I

think. I had to stay with the crew after I pulled you out of the fire."

She blinked. "Yeah, about that. How did you get to Three Lakes so fast? I thought you were in Newberry."

He grimaced and looked away, his lips drawn into a tight line. "I was when you called. I, uh, I flew here to Three Lakes."

"Flew?" She frowned. "As in drove really fast?"

He shook his head. "No, flew, as in flight."

"In a plane?"

He shook his head again and took a deep breath. "No. Under my own power." He lowered his voice and leaned closer. "What do you remember about the fire? Did you see anything unusual?"

She raised an eyebrow. "Unusual? While the room was burning around me and smoke was clouding my vision? Why would I see anything unusual?"

He opened his mouth to say something, but the door behind him swung open and a woman who looked like a Peruvian princess strode in, a stethoscope looped around her neck.

"Good evening, Ms. Three-Hearts, I'm Doctor Cantora. How are you feeling?"

Estelle relaxed a little, offering a watery smile. "I'm okay, Doctor. Better than being in a burning building, for sure."

Dr. Cantora's eyes crinkled as she smiled. "Yes, I would agree. The good news is you're going to be fine. You're a little dehydrated and have a few first degree burns on your hands. And your throat's fairly raw from the smoke inhalation, but in a few days you're going to be fine."

Estelle nodded. "Okay. It sounds like I got off lucky."

"Yes, I do believe so. But sometimes it's good to have a guardian to watch out for us, yes?" Dr. Cantora winked. "I'd like to keep you overnight to make sure your lungs recover from the smoke inhalation, but tomorrow you'll be able to go home."

"Thanks, Doctor."

"You're welcome. Merry Christmas." The doctor patted the bed before she headed out the door, leaving them alone.

"Sounds like I'm going to be okay." Estelle scanned Mark's face, wondering why he didn't look relieved. "How about you? Are you going to be okay?"

He sighed and rubbed the back of his neck. "Shit." He met her gaze and opened his mouth to speak, but thought better of it and rose. "Hold that thought." He stepped away from the bed and looked out from behind the door, evidently searching for the doctor. When he saw nothing amiss, he ducked back in and closed it behind him. He returned to his seat, but unease still wreathed his face.

"Okay, this is going to sound weird, but it's the truth, and there's really no way to break this to you gently."

"What are you talking about?"

"I'm a Firebird."

Estelle blinked, trying to sort out the words into something that made sense. "Is that the name of your nation?"

"No, Estelle. A Firebird, the mythical flaming bird that's said to bring about a cataclysmic change in the world? That's me. I'm a Firebird."

She wanted to laugh, to wave his statements away, but he wasn't smiling. His expression remained serious.

"Wait, wait. A Firebird, seriously? Come on, those only exist in the stories."

Mark grimaced and nodded. "Yes, they're in the stories, but every story has a grain of truth. It just happens the truth is the Firebird. And I'm one of them." He rubbed his hands on his thighs. "That's how I got from Newberry to Three Lakes so fast. I flew here in my natural form."

It was too much and she grinned. "Come on. Seriously?"

He sighed and her gut cramped as he shot one more look around. "Yes, seriously."

He held out his hand palm up and closed his eyes. One moment there was an open, human palm with smooth skin, and the next the number of fingers dropped to three and turned to black-clawed talons. Flames contained in a burning orb hovered just above the scaled palm, flickering with light and heat.

She gasped and jerked away from the flames, her throat closing as fear lurched from her gut. *Holy shit, he's a Firebird!* Panic made her moan and tears slid down her cheeks. She'd been with a mythical beast the whole time. *Sweet glory, I had sex with him!* But he looked so human, and seemed so normal.

"Oh my glory." She couldn't stop staring at his hand as the flames died and the five fingers appeared unharmed. "Oh my glory. Please, don't hurt me. I didn't know you were real. I thought it was just a dream. I didn't know you actually existed."

"Oh, Estelle—" He reached for her hand, but she yanked it away and leaned farther back. He pulled his hand to his lap. "I'd never hurt you. I couldn't. I, um, I'm bound to you."

"What?"

"Yeah." He nodded, his expression sad. "When we made love, I accidentally bonded with you, as my mate. For life." He straightened his shoulders and sighed. "I couldn't hurt you and I'll always protect you. The Goddess chose you as my mate and we bonded during our intimacy. That little mark on your hip that looks like a bird. That's the mark of bonded mates."

She stared at him, searching her memory for any new marks on her body. Had she seen the one he was talking about? She frowned. She had observed something on her hip, but she thought it was a mole or a birthmark she'd never noticed.

"You marked me?"

"Not on purpose. It's a sacred thing among the Elder Races, particularly the Thunderbird families."

"I thought you said you're a Firebird."

He nodded, his shoulders slumped. "I am. One in every two million Thunderbirds is born a Firebird. My twin brother is a Thunderbird."

"Wait, back up." She shook her head. "It's a sacred thing to mark your mate, but you didn't mean to with me. And you're from a race of mythical creatures, and now I'm bonded to you? Forever?"

He looked like he wanted to give her a drawn-out explanation, but he only nodded. "Yes."

Sweet glory.

Estelle couldn't get her mind around anything he'd told her. She was human and he wasn't, but they were now bonded as mates, if he could be believed. *He lit his frickin' palm on fire. I think I can believe him.* But it didn't make any sense. The stories were meant as teaching fables, an entertaining way to convey morality and the rules of the people. Such creatures weren't supposed to exist. Not outside of the tales.

Oh, dear Goddess, I have to get out of here.

"Estelle? Say something, please." Mark wore misery and concern like a cloak, his shoulders tight with tension. His beautiful eyes pleaded with her to believe and understand.

I can't.

"My throat's really dry. Do you think you could find me some hot tea with honey and lemon?"

"Of course." He rose to his feet, his gaze on her. "Are you going to be okay?"

"Yeah, I'll be fine."

He nodded slowly, his lips tight, but he retreated from her room into the main part of the clinic.

As soon as the door closed, she threw off the covers

and tugged the oxygen tube from her nose and the IV from her arm. She used the sheet from the bed to stop the bleeding from her elbow as she searched for her clothes. They'd piled them on the chair and she could smell them across the room. It didn't matter. She just had to get out of here, now.

She shoved her legs into her jeans and her arms into her sweater before she sat to yank on her socks and shoes. A few times she thought she heard voices outside her room and paused, her heart hammering in her chest. But no one came in and she finished dressing with economy of motion. Her hands ached in the bandages from the burns, but she'd deal with that later. *Lavender oil.* If she still had some. She grasped her laptop bag and her camera before she crept to the door and cracked it open.

No one stood in the hallway outside. Taking a deep breath, she slipped through and closed the door softly behind her. She probably couldn't go out the front without someone noticing her. The clinic sat mostly empty given the holiday and the time of night. Most people were "nestled all snug in their beds" or sipping hot cocoa in front of a fire while their trees twinkled with lights.

She could've been celebrating with the firefighters of Newberry if she hadn't been so stupid to go into her studio first. She would've been on the road instead of caught in a fire. Shaking her head to get rid of the condemnation, she skittered toward the back of the clinic. They had to have an emergency exit, or a place where the ambulances could drop off patients in more critical conditions. While not a true emergency room, the clinic did have some remarkable triage equipment and staff.

Estelle found the entrance to the ambulance drop-off and ducked through the sliding doors, keeping her head down just in case someone checked the security camera footage later. She didn't want to be there when Mark came back.

Oh glory, Mark. What did she do about that? He wasn't human, and she'd had sex with him. He could generate fire in his palm, for the Goddess' sake. And now he said she was bound to him. What the hell did that really mean?

She pulled up the hood on her jacket as she crossed Main Street in front of the clinic. While her home lay on the same side as the clinic, she didn't want anyone to look out and see her walking. She had to get home, to get to her studio, to think.

She'd made it to the block containing the Ironwood Café when she realized she didn't have a home or a studio. The fire had consumed everything she owned in one blazing night. *What about my Jeep?* It had been parked in the residents' lot behind the building. Had the fire consumed that as well? Estelle stopped dead on the sidewalk. *Oh glory, where am I going to go? I don't even have a home anymore.*

The loss hit her like a load of bricks and she stood, stumped, in the middle of the sidewalk. Everything was gone. She had nothing left.

"Estelle? Are you all right?"

She raised her head and met the worried gaze of Iris Maple, the owner of the Ironwood Café. She opened her mouth, but nothing came out, and she could only shake her head.

"Sweet branches of the Home Tree, you look like you could use something hot to drink." Iris peered into her face. "Come inside with me. It's too cold out here to stay for long." The tall woman waved her toward the door of the Ironwood and Estelle didn't have the energy to protest.

Once inside the darkened room, Iris flipped on the lights and Estelle was momentarily struck dumb at the beauty around her. It looked like a winter wonderland with lights woven into the branches of fir and pine, and glass icicles hanging from them to reflect the light. The tree-beams had been painted white to give the impression of cozy winter, and some of her panicked tension released.

"Glory, this place is always so beautiful inside." She hadn't meant to say the words aloud, but Iris beamed and nodded.

"Thank you. Ben thinks it's over the top, but he indulges me to do the decorating like this. It makes me happy, and he says that makes him happy." She gestured to one of the booths along the white painted brick wall. "Take a seat and rest. I'll bring the cocoa."

"Thanks."

Estelle settled into the booth and closed her eyes, trying to find the calm she usually possessed. But the images of the flames licking the walls of her studio and the fear of being trapped and burned to death swallowed her equanimity. Another image of Mark's hand turning to black talons and flames made the tears slide down her cheeks without an end in sight.

"Oh, now, don't cry. It'll be all right." Iris's sweet voice broke Estelle's reverie and she looked for a napkin to wipe her face. "What's got you all worked up tonight?"

Estelle shook her head. "My home and my studio burned to the ground tonight. I've lost everything."

"Oh, seedling, I'm so sorry to hear that." Iris tilted her head with a small frown. "You weren't inside, were you?"

Estelle nodded. "Mark Redfeather rescued me."

"Oh, thank the Goddess you made it out. How terribly frightening." Iris gripped her wrist. "I'm sorry you lost your studio and home, but I'm so glad you're all right. Where's Mark? Did he have to do more work with the firefighters?"

"No. He was at the clinic with me."

Iris blinked. "Then why are you out here wandering around in the darkness at this hour?"

"Because he's not human!" Tears kept coming in waves and she couldn't stop them. "He's not human. He's a mythical creature from the Peoples' legends. He's a Firebird, and he says he's bound to me as his mate. But none of this makes sense and I'm human, and I don't have a home to go to. I don't know what to do, but I don't understand how I'm human and he's not, and…"

Iris let her cry for a few moments before she reached across the table to rest her hand on Estelle's. "Did he say he's not human?"

She nodded. "And he showed me. He made a ball of flames in his hand."

Iris nodded as well. "Let me get the cocoa, and we'll talk more about this." She slid out of the booth and disappeared into the kitchen while Estelle tried to get her emotions under control.

What am I going to do?

She had no home, she had no studio, and she didn't have anywhere to go. She couldn't go to Newberry and hang out with the firefighters. Maybe she could visit her brother. But he had enough issues without his sister crashing at his place. Where could she go?

She hadn't come up with any viable options when Iris returned with two steaming mugs of thick, rich cocoa. She set them down on the table before she slid into the booth.

"Oh, seedling, it's going to be okay. We'll work it out. I know you've experienced a lot tonight, but it will improve. Have some chocolate. Chocolate makes everything better."

Estelle snorted, but couldn't quite smile. "Yeah." She sipped her hot drink as instructed and fell into the rich flavor. *Damn, this is the best hot cocoa I've ever had.*

"I hope you don't mind, but I called someone I think can help you with your dilemma better than I can. She helps everyone who needs it, and she has a unique perspective that matches yours." Iris gave her a contrite smile. "I don't want to take liberties, but I also don't feel like I can offer you the best advice."

Estelle swallowed hard and tried not to cry again. "Who did you call?"

"Kate Blackamber. She's on her way here."

Estelle's heart sank. "Oh glory, you disturbed her on Christmas Eve? No, no, no. I don't want to make anyone's holiday suck as much as mine."

"Easy, Estelle. It's just a day. This celebration can happen any time at the end of December." Iris squeezed her arm with gentle firmness. "The specific day doesn't really matter as long as there's love and connection. And Kate's great at love and connection. She's a master."

"I'm not trying to mess everything up. I just don't know what to do."

"I know." Iris nodded and sipped her own chocolate. "Sometimes you need the wisdom of others just so you can find your own path. Kate's great at helping people."

"I'm not sure she can help with this."

Estelle settled into the booth and her mug of cocoa, allowing the warmth to seep into her despair and take the edge off. She closed her eyes, recognizing she was being rude to Iris, but she didn't have the energy to face the music just yet. *I don't know what Kate thinks she can do, but at the moment, there's nothing I can do.*

It didn't take long for Kate to come in, but Estelle still hadn't found the solace she sought. Her heart ached for the loss from the fire, but also the loss of the man she'd fallen for. *Sweet Goddess, I'm in love with a mythical beast.*

"Hey, Estelle. Iris said you were in trouble. What's going on?" Kate pulled up a chair and settled into it as Iris brought her a mug of chocolate. "Thanks, Iris."

Estelle raised her gaze to meet Kate's and wished she knew what to say. "There was a fire tonight."

"Oh no. Was anyone hurt?"

Estelle shook her head. "No, well, not really. I almost died in it, but I'm okay."

"Oh my glory! How did you get out?"

"Mark Redfeather." Estelle's throat closed on his name. "He…he came and pulled me out."

"That's great." Kate paused, scanning her face. "Isn't it?"

The tears returned. "It would be if he was human." Estelle closed her eyes and dropped her head to the table, the pain and sorrow stealing her breath between sobs.

"Whoa, okay. Now I understand why Iris called me." Kate's voice sounded above Estelle as she moved to her side. "Scooch over a little and let me sit next to you."

Estelle moved enough to let Kate into the booth, but she didn't raise her head.

"I bet that was a lot to take in, huh? How did he show you he wasn't human?"

Estelle sniffed hard and took the napkin Iris handed her to wipe her nose. "He made a ball of flame in his hand. And his hand turned into a three-fingered talon from a bird."

"Yeah, that would do it for me, too."

"I didn't know what to do so I ducked out of the clinic to find a place to think. But my house and studio burned down. I don't have anywhere to go."

"Now, that's not true. You're here, right now, drinking this fantastic chocolate from the Ironwood Café, and you're not being chased by monsters, so I'm pretty sure that's a step in the right direction." Kate grinned.

Estelle shot her a flat look. "I think Mark could qualify as a monster."

"Maybe, if you don't understand who and what he really is. There are more things in heaven and earth than are dreamt of in your philosophy, Horatio." Kate bumped her shoulder a little. "Has he ever hurt you, deliberately, with this non-human ability of his?"

Estelle shook her head. "No, he said he couldn't. He said we'd bonded when…" She shot a look at the others and decided to leave the detail out. "He said we were mates and he'd never be able to hurt his mate."

"Oh boy. And you mated before he told you what he was?"

Estelle shrugged. "I guess so. He said it was an accident."

"The mating?"

"The mating before telling, I guess."

"Ah, yeah." Kate nodded and took a sip of her chocolate. "I can see how that might make things difficult, for both of you." She shook her head and laughed with a rueful edge to her voice. "I pretty much had the exact same experience."

Estelle blinked and raised her head. "You did? How?"

Kate laughed again. "Jayson showed up here in Three Lakes and told me we were true mates, even though I'd only met him once at my best friend's wedding. I thought he was crazy when he told me he was a werewolf."

Estelle's jaw dropped. "A werewolf?"

"Yup. An Alpha werewolf and retired Navy SEAL. I damn near lost my mind when he chased me down, literally." Kate shook her head with a rueful smile. "Turns out, he was right, but he was pretty upfront about the whole mating-for-life thing. He was terrified I wouldn't understand and would deny him. Which meant he was on the hook forever to a person who was either afraid of or repulsed by him, but he wouldn't be able to be with anyone else. It was a mess for a while."

Estelle shook her head. "How can you be so calm about him being a werewolf? Or Mark being a Firebird? I can't get my head around it. That they even exist."

Kate nodded again and sipped her chocolate as she shared a glance with Iris. "Here's the thing. These beings have been here the whole time. Humans just never noticed them. Their camouflage is so good, we think of them as people. And they are people, just not the human variety." She paused, rubbing her chin. "To be honest, the worst monsters I've ever met in my life weren't from the Elder Races. They were human. One of them tried to kill me two years ago and another tried to kill a friend of mine."

"What?" Estelle rocked back, scanning the other woman beside her. "Are you serious?"

"Yup. And you know who saved my life?" Kate tilted her head and raised her eyebrows. "A werewolf and the other members of the Elder Races community here." She sat back and stared Estelle down. "These people are very powerful and some of them are very long lived. But they aren't the monsters they're made out to be, and they fear humans for the same reasons humans fear them."

Estelle licked her lips and swallowed. "I'm waiting for you to say they're just like you and me, some good, some bad, etc."

"I didn't think I needed to." Kate gave her a thoughtful smile. "You seem smart enough and wise enough to see beyond what you've been taught to believe. Give Mark a chance. He's a Firebird and your mate, but he's more than that. He's an honorable and loving man who knows in his heart you're the only one for him. How many human men know that?"

None in Estelle's experience. But could she love a man who had a duel nature?

Don't be stupid. You already love him.

The revelation hit her like a two-by-four up against her head. She loved him. She had for a while now, though she couldn't pinpoint the moment it started. Was it when she helped him with the dishes at the fire station? Was it when he posed for pictures in the calendar for her pet cause? Was it when he helped out with the second day of the photoshoot? She didn't know, but each of those times had brought to her how much she wanted to be with him more.

And now he tells me his greatest secret and I run out of the clinic like the Hounds of Hell are on my tail.

"Ugh, you're right, Kate. Mark's not the monster. I

am." She covered her face with her hands as she came to terms with the truth. "I just hurt him so badly. He told me his secret and I ran away." She heard Iris get up and head for the kitchen while Kate sighed.

"Yeah, that might put a hitch in your giddy-up. But I told you I ran from a werewolf, right?"

"Right."

"Who's now my husband. Right?"

"Right." Estelle dropped her hands.

"Guess what he did?" Kate gave her a smirk.

"What?"

"He chased me down and didn't give up on me. He even gave me the time to figure out what the hell I needed to do to come to terms with this." Kate sipped the last of her chocolate from the mug. "Here's the thing. Once they know their true mates, werewolves never give up on that person. I suspect Firebirds might be the same. He'll give you the time to figure it out. But I'm betting you can cut the time down by at least ninety percent if you tell him where you are and that you want to talk."

Estelle nodded. "Yeah, I need to call him."

Iris returned to the table with three steaming mugs of tea. "It's peppermint since it's the time of year for candy canes and snow."

"Oh yeah, peppermint tea is perfect." Kate smiled and wrapped her hands around a new mug. "It's really pretty in here, Iris. It's very festive."

"Thank you, Kate. Ben wasn't as excited about the decorations, but he seems to like them once they're up." Iris raised her head and ran her gaze over the ceiling. "It makes me happy in the season of sleep."

"I can see why." Kate turned her gaze on Estelle. "Why don't you text Mark? Then we can enjoy our tea until he gets here."

Estelle nodded as she pulled out her phone. The question was, would he agree to speak to her?

CHAPTER TWELVE

Mark stared at the empty hospital bed and his stomach took a nosedive. *She's gone.* He understood his dual nature would be a lot for Estelle to take in, but he didn't think she'd run. The handle of the mug cracked as his fist tightened and he had to set it down on a nearby ledge before he dropped it.

Sorrow greater than when his family retreated ripped through him, draining his heart and soul until he felt nothing but pain and emptiness. Estelle's retreat tore his heart out and he felt numb. He wasn't sure he'd ever breathe again. She was his mate. He'd already bonded to her. But with her disappearance, he'd lost the direction he needed to go. *Oh, Goddess, what do I do now?*

"Mr. Redfeather? Is everything all right?"

Dr. Cantora's voice intruded on his numbness, returning him to the world of light.

"She's gone." The words tore from his chest.

"Who? Ms. Three-Hearts?" The doctor stepped around him and looked at the empty bed. "Oh dear. Do you have any idea where she might go?"

"Uh…" He dragged his mind away from the morass of pain and tried to organize his thoughts. "I don't. Her apartment and studio burned to the ground tonight, so she can't go home."

"Does she have any family nearby?" Dr. Cantora swung out of the room and headed for the reception area. "Is there anyone we can call?"

"I don't know. She has a brother, but I think he's in Newberry. And her uncle is the captain of the fire station, but he's helping with the fire tonight." Mark shook his head. "I don't know where she'd go."

"Okay, let's slow down here. Let me call the sheriff and ask him to keep an eye out for her." She picked up the phone and dialed a number. "What would make her take off like that?"

Guilt, sorrow, and anger flashed through him, but he kept his lips shut on his teeth while the doctor talked to Sheriff Boulderson. He could scent the doctor's otherness as he had on the sheriff. How could Estelle live in this town and not know that the Elder Races made up damn near half of it? Hell, Kate Blackamber was *Morukai*, for the Goddess' sake.

"Okay, thanks, Sheriff." Dr. Cantora hung up the phone. "He says he'll keep a lookout for her while on patrol tonight. It just started snowing and the temperature's dropping. Not a good night to be out without shelter."

"It's my fault she's out there."

"What?" Dr. Cantora raised her eyebrows.

"It's my fault she's out in the snow." He shot a look at the nurse and closed his mouth with a grimace.

Dr. Cantora followed his gaze and nodded. "Let's go back to my office where you can relax a little. Here." She reached for the teapot and a paper to-go cup. "Let's take some tea with us."

She filled two cups and led him back to her office. He stepped inside and settled into one of the chairs as she closed the door behind him.

"All right, tell me why you think it's your fault Ms.

Three-Hearts left the clinic."

"She's human, and I told her I'm not."

Dr. Cantora raised her chin and took a deep breath in. "Oh."

"Yeah. But I didn't have a choice. I mated with her, bonded, and I couldn't hide it from her. She needed to know." He grimaced and shook his head. "It wasn't intentional, but the Firebird in me knew she was the one, and took the decision out of my hands."

"Oh dear." Dr. Cantora rubbed her chin. "She wasn't aware of the Elder Races before tonight?"

He shook his head. "No."

"Oh dear." She shoved a cup of tea across her desk to him. "Take some tea and let me think. I'm not sure going after her is the best idea, but she can't stay out in the snow."

She tapped her chin while Mark sipped the tea. While it didn't solve everything, it definitely eased some of his hurt. *I've really fucked up this time.* He didn't often make mistakes, but this one definitely qualified.

"Let me call Kate Blackamber. If anyone would know what to do about this, it's her." Dr. Cantora tilted her head. "You know Kate's our *Morukai*?"

"Yes, ma'am. I got to meet her about a week ago. She's not what I expected."

Dr. Cantora laughed. "No, she never has been. But I think that's because she grew up thinking she was human, and had no knowledge of her heritage or the Elder Races."

"What?" Mark raised his eyebrows. "Are you serious?"

"Oh yeah. Can you imagine what happened when she first met her husband and he said he was a werewolf?" Dr. Cantora grinned. "As I understand it, it took a lot of coaxing and explaining before she let him anywhere near her."

Despite his sorrow, Mark grinned. "Yeah, I bet it

didn't go well." He lost his smile. "Like it didn't go well with me tonight."

"Don't give up, Mr. Redfeather." Dr. Cantora picked up her phone. "If the Goddess picked Ms. Three-Hearts as your mate, it will work out. She doesn't make mistakes, but that doesn't mean it's an easy road. Just keep on keeping on, and everything will settle into place."

Mark nodded, but his heart felt too heavy to believe her words. She wasn't wrong about the Goddess, but at the moment, things looked pretty grim. He sipped his tea, wishing the heat would ease some of the numbness. He didn't often mute his fire, but Estelle's retreat had thrown snow on his inner hearth.

"Okay, thanks, Jayson." Dr. Cantora hung up the phone. "Good news, Mr. Redfeather. Kate's already on the job."

"What?"

"Yes, apparently Iris Maple found Ms. Three-Hearts walking in town and brought her to the Ironwood Café, then called Kate." She rose from behind her desk. "They're there right now. Would you like me to give you a ride?"

He rose as well, gripping the cup to absorb the heat as hope bloomed. "No, thank you, Dr. Cantora. I think I better walk. I will give me some time to plan my approach."

The doctor gifted him with a brilliant smile. "That's a great way to think of it, Mr. Redfeather." She held out her hand and gripped his wrist when he took it. "I wish you luck and heart. With Kate, great things always happen. Blessings."

"Thanks for your help tonight, Doctor."

"Make sure she uses lavender oil on those burns and gets plenty of fluids." Dr. Cantora gave him a stern look, ruined by the twinkle in her eyes.

"Yes, ma'am. I'll try." He nodded with the beginnings of a smile for the first time that night. *It might work out.*

He left her office and strode toward the doors of the

clinic, zipping his borrowed coat as he went. *With Kate, great things always happen.* The doctor's words buoyed up his spirit and he took a deep breath. *This can be fixed.* He just had to find the right state of mind. His grandmother's face filled his mind with the amused patience she always wore when he'd rushed into things. *Go slow and patient, grandson. Hot coals last longer than a grassfire.*

Cold, wet snow hit him as soon as he stepped out from under the vestibule at the clinic, and his phone vibrated in his pocket. He ignored it, not wishing to take off his gloves to see who it was. He paused and scanned the world around him as his breathing settled. Everything sat under a thin white blanket of snow, and the peace and silence of the world settled some of his worries. No one seemed to be out in the weather except him, but he appreciated the stillness and the solitude. He needed both to find a way to talk to Estelle and convince her his love and his devotion wouldn't hurt her.

How do you convince a human not to fear the mythical creatures?

His gut clenched as he crossed the street and turned his feet toward the Ironwood Café. Maybe he wouldn't have to. Maybe Kate would lay the groundwork for Estelle to understand he wasn't the monster of the fables she'd grown up with. *That's a lot to expect from a woman you barely know.* But the doctor had said great things happened around Kate, and she was the *Morukai* Shaman, Speaker for the Goddess. *Maybe it's time to renew my own faith.*

Mark arrived at the doors of the Ironwood Café and paused to take a deep breath. *It's now or never.* The lights beckoned from within with a warmth he craved and he couldn't resist their allure. He pulled the door open and stepped inside.

Heat blasted over him and stole some of his tension along with the cold. He scanned the room and found three women watching him from a booth against the brick wall.

Kate and Iris gave him a warm smile, but his gaze riveted to Estelle, who bit her lip in concern. He tried to smile away her worries as he wove through the tables to theirs and stopped.

"Good evening, Mr. Redfeather. Would you like some tea?" Iris rose, a serene smile curling her lips. "Take my spot and sit down. I'll bring the pot for you to enjoy." She sauntered away toward the kitchen before Mark could say a word.

"Hey, Mark. Good to see you." Kate scooted out of the booth and stood before turning to Estelle. "Good talk tonight, Estelle. Thanks for sharing the tea with me, but I gotta get going. I want to spend some time with Jayson on Christmas Eve. You gonna be okay?"

"Yes, thank you, Kate. I really appreciate it."

Kate beamed. "You're welcome." She turned to Mark. "She's all yours. Good luck." She winked before she zipped up her coat. "Thanks for the tea, Iris!"

Mark didn't see where she went after that. His gaze was locked on Estelle as he slid into the booth across from her, his heart pounding in his chest. Neither of them said anything as Iris returned to the table with a pot of the fragrant peppermint tea and a fresh mug.

"There you go. Let me take these dirties out of the way for you."

"Thanks, Iris." Estelle briefly looked up with a smile, but it faded as the proprietor left them alone. She bit her lip and swallowed hard, but didn't say anything more.

Time to make the first move.

"I'm sorry."

To his surprise, they said it at the same time, and both grinned at their overlapping apologies.

"You go first." He wrapped his hands around the mug to keep from touching her.

"I'm so sorry, Mark." She rubbed her fingers with her opposite hand as she held her mug. "I didn't understand,

and I didn't react well."

"It's a lot to take in." He gave her a one-shouldered shrug. "I kinda sprung it on you."

She looked away and shook her head. "Maybe, but there are more things in heaven and earth than are dreamt of in my philosophy, and I'm apparently on the fast track to learn them."

"By quoting Shakespeare?"

She shrugged again. "That's how Kate said it, but she wasn't wrong. To be brutally honest, humans are stupid and arrogant to think they're the only upright and sentient beings in the world. And I've known since I was old enough to walk how humans treat those they perceive as different. Having the look and heritage of the First Peoples will do that."

He nodded, thinking it wiser to stay silent.

"So, I'm sorry I couldn't see beyond my own fear to remember the person you are and the way you've always treated me. The flaming ball was a new trick." She shot him a rueful smirk and he grunted a laugh. "But you've never hurt me and except for telling me what you are, you've always been honest with me. And I can understand why you didn't disclose your true nature earlier." She grimaced. "Humans are stupid."

"Okay, stop." He couldn't resist and reached for one of her hands. Gratitude filled him when she didn't pull away. "A fire just took away your apartment and your studio, and then your lover throws you the biggest curve ball ever. I think you're entitled to a little 'stupidity' reaction."

She snorted, but sorrow filled her face. "I'm sorry."

He nodded. "I won't say it didn't hurt, because to be honest, it felt like you ripped my heart out and stomped on it. But a part of me understands why you reacted the way you did. You're human and as far as you were taught, the myths of your people were just that, myths. To have the veil ripped away would be terrifying."

She shook her head. "That doesn't mean I should ignore what I know about you."

"Maybe not, but how long have you known me? At most, two weeks? It's a short time, even in human terms." He tried to smile around the pain. "My people are given the blessing from the Goddess to know our mates the moment we meet them. I didn't expect to find a human woman as remarkable as you to be my mate, and I really didn't mean to bond with you before you understood what I am. But I am bound to you and you are my mate, and I will never hurt you. And I will wait for you as long as I have to because of that. I'll never give up on you."

To his horror, her face crumpled and tears flooded down her cheeks. *Aw hell, now what do I do?* But instead of folding in on herself, Estelle scooted out from her side of the booth and slid in beside him, throwing her arms around him. He twisted enough to wrap his own arms around her and cuddled her close, her scent settling his Firebird better than the tea.

"You promise? You'll wait for me to figure this out?"

"I will if you give me a chance, if you don't give up on me."

"Oh glory, Mark. I won't give up on you. I want to be with you. I love you."

I love you.

The words slammed into him, reverberating around his head like a claxon. She loved him. He couldn't speak from the explosions of relief and hope filling his head and chest. His Firebird screamed in triumph and jubilation. He held her close and closed his eyes to take in the warmth she offered him, healing his bleeding heart from the inside out.

"I love you, too, Estelle. Please give me the chance to show you. Please spend Christmas and New Year's, and every other holiday with me. I need you." He hadn't meant to say the last, but the truth wouldn't stay behind his teeth. He needed her to fill the hole in his heart, to find the connection he'd been missing since his grandmother died. *You sent her to me, didn't you,* nei'eibehe'? *This was your parting gift, wasn't it?*

No words came to him, but his grandmother's full and booming laughter rang out in his mind, and he couldn't help but smile. Hohou, nei'eibehe'. *Thank you, Grandmother.*

"I'll be here with you. How about we work on this thing together, with complete honesty?" Estelle sat back and smiled up at him.

"I think that's a fantastic idea. Can we start tonight?"

She nodded, but her smile died. "But where? My apartment and studio are gone." She bit her lip as if to stop from crying. He scrambled to find something happy to talk about.

"Let's go to Newberry like we planned." He nudged her to get up and she slid out of the booth. "I'm pretty sure the captain would like us both to be there. Me, because I'm working, technically, and you because you're family."

"And how are we gonna get there, smart guy? Are you going to fly me there? Because I'm not exactly flame-resistant here." She gave him a smirk to show she teased.

"I think it would be wiser to take your Jeep."

"My Jeep?" Her eyes widened. "It didn't burn to a crisp with the building?"

"Nope. I dug the keys out of your pocket when they loaded you in to the ambulance and drove it to the clinic when I came to see you." He frowned. "You didn't see it in the parking lot when you snuck out?"

She had the grace to blush. "No, I didn't. I wasn't thinking very clearly." She raised her chin and straightened her shoulders. "I'm ready to go. I really want to be with family this year." She waved at Iris who came out to see them off. "Thank you for the help and the tea, Iris. What do I owe you?"

Iris smiled and waved her hand dismissively. "It's on

the house. Take care of each other, please. Life is too long to be alone."

Ain't that the truth.

Iris locked the doors behind them as Estelle thrust her arm through his. "Family. That's what I want for Christmas this year."

"Your uncle will be happy to see you." He ignored the disappointment that he wasn't yet her family.

She nodded as they crossed the street, leaving footprints in the snow. "I'm sure he will, but he's not the family I was referring to." She looked up at him with her pale eyes shining the holiday lights hanging overhead. "I meant you. I want you to be part of my family. I want you to be with me this Christmas. I want you."

He couldn't stop the happy grin stretching his lips. "You have me, for all time and all holidays, *beebeenei. Biixoothethen.*"

She tilted her head. "What does that mean?"

"I love you, straight from my Arapaho heart."

She smiled. "Kindle my heart's flame with yours, Mark. Because I love you, too."

Oh, he'd kindle more than that, but for now, that was good enough.

EPILOGUE

"Happy birthday!"

The cheer echoed through the fire station as the Newberry firefighters raised their glasses of sparkling cider to the New Year and to Estelle's and Mark's birthdays. Estelle raised her own glass with a big smile and a sense of belonging. The week after the fire took her home and studio had been a busy one, but she'd been glad for the distraction.

The fire had been labeled arson and the investigator had found multiple places where accelerant had been used to ignite the flames. Apparently, Crichton Duckworth had been up to his ears in gambling debts to the Detroit contingent of the Irish Mob, and thought the insurance money would help him pay them back. He thought everyone would be gone on Christmas Eve and timed the fire for when the building was supposed to be empty. Except it wasn't. Now he was being charged with arson and attempted homicide. Seemed like a fitting end to him.

Because Estelle had managed to rescue her laptop, the calendar had come out on time and the sales were through the roof. As predicted, the highest sales came from the over-fifty set, and reports came back it was because of the

Silver Fox Santa image. Estelle had to admit it was one of the best she'd taken that year.

"To Estelle and Mark, may it be the happiest year yet." Uncle Jeff grinned as he handed out a few little gifts to everyone.

"Wait a minute, it's our birthday, why is everyone else getting gifts?" Mark shot the captain a mock-frown while his eyes twinkled.

"Because none of us got to have a Christmas, so we're doing a two-fer celebration." Mayfair handed out chocolate candies in the shape of trees to everyone in the room. "Besides, Estelle's gift is the best."

"Shhh!" Several of the others hissed at Mayfair and he ducked his head as Estelle raised her eyebrows.

"My gift?"

"Yeah, you know, the calendars." Torrington took up the explanation. "Every one of us got one because damn, we do look good. Best gift ever."

"Oh, right." That sounded plausible enough, but the way Uncle Jeff bumped fists with Torrington made her think she still missed something.

"All right, let's open these gifts before the bell rings and some idiot lights their home on fire."

Everyone laughed and dug into the little brightly wrapped packages. Estelle sat back beside Mark and watched, grateful to be in the company of family. *My family.* The firefighters would remain an extended family, particularly as long as Uncle Jeff led them. But Mark would always be her home and heart. *Or hearth as the case may be.* The man was hot and not just because of his Firebird heritage. He could warm her bed anytime.

"How are you doing?" Mark leaned over and brushed a kiss long her cheek.

"Good. Really good." She smiled at him as she cuddled against his warm body. "Happy to be with you. Happy birthday, *hookesiteeno.*"

"Happy birthday to you, *beebeenei*. I love sharing it with you."

"Yeah, me too. Let's do this every year, okay?"

"Sounds like a plan."

"Okay, break it up over there, you lovebirds." Uncle Jeff waved a thick manila envelope at them as he grinned. "You really should get a room if you're going to show that much public display of affection."

Estelle laughed, though sorrow hit her with the memory of her lost apartment and studio. "I would, but it burned down in Three Lakes."

"Yeah." Uncle Jeff nodded, his eyes narrowing. "About that." He handed her the envelope and waited expectantly.

"What's this?"

"Open it."

She grinned in the face of his obvious excitement. He looked like a little boy who'd found his mom the best gift ever. She shot a look at Mark, but he seemed just as surprised as her.

Estelle peeled open the top flap and tugged out a sheaf of papers. On the top read "Deed to Land", and below that gave the details. She read a few moments, trying to comprehend what she was looking at.

"What is this?" She looked back up at her uncle. "Did you buy me some land?"

"Not exactly." He shot a glance around at the others and they grinned back at him. "The guys and I wanted to do something special for your birthday since you went to all the trouble to make the calendars. That land has a small house and a garage with a workshop on it. It's been in our family for a long time and I thought you could use it for a home and a photography studio. So, I've signed the deed to it over to you and the guys pooled some money together to furnish it."

He grinned and shrugged. "It's not fancy, but it's

livable, especially at this time of year."

"Oh my glory." Estelle threw a wide-eye look at Mark. "Did you know about this?"

He shook his head, surprise on his face. "No, ma'am. But if I had, I would've gone in on it." He narrowed his eyes at the captain.

"Hey, now, it's your birthday, too. So, this is for you." The captain handed him his own envelope.

Mark took it and slit it open with his fingers, pulling out a tri-folded piece of paper. Estelle leaned over to see what it was.

"It's an open-ended plane ticket to visit your family since you had to miss your grandmother's memorial." Uncle Jeff shrugged a little. "This time of year makes it tough to travel, especially with the weather. We bought a ticket that can be changed at any time so you can go visit." He nodded toward Estelle. "And take anyone along with you who might want to go." Jeff winked.

"Wow, I don't know what to say." Mark gaped at his friends and colleagues.

"I think it's customary to say 'thank you'." She elbowed him gently.

They all laughed and Mark grinned. "Thaaaannnkk yyoooooouuu."

"Good job." She patted his shoulder and ducked as he swiped at her. "Yes, thank you all very much. Such generous gifts. I really appreciate it." She opened the deed again. "Where is this land located?"

Jeff reached for the bundle of papers and pulled out a photocopied map. "It's about two miles outside of Three Lakes on a half mile square plot of land near that sharp bend in Road 500. We figured you could set up your studio there and not be too far from town."

"Wow, that's wonderful." She shook the envelope and a set of keys fell into her hand. "I even have keys already."

"Oh yeah. The only thing you'll need are groceries.

The rest of the place is move-in ready."

Estelle rose and threw herself into her uncle's arms. "Thank you very much."

"You're welcome." He laughed and squeezed her gently. "Happy birthday."

She pulled back and kissed his cheek before she turned to Mark. "Want to go grocery shopping?"

****

Mark settled back on the couch in Estelle's new house as the snow started to fall again in earnest. A fire crackled in the fireplace and heated the main room with cheery light. His Firebird bathed in the closeness of its element as he watched Estelle wipe down her new kitchen counters and settle onto the couch with a mug of tea. The cake they'd bought at the grocery store in Newberry sat between them on the coffee table, with two candles lying beside the plate.

"Ready to light the candles and make a wish?" She gestured to the cake with a smile.

"Not quite yet." He reached for her mug and set it on the table beside the cake. "Come sit with me a moment." He tugged her to him, her back against his chest. "Comfortable?"

"Yeah." She wiggled a bit to find the best position then relaxed. "Yeah. I'm very comfortable."

"Good."

They sat that way a few moments, listening to the fire crackle. Mark closed his eyes and focused on the sounds, smells, and textures of the moment. He had his mate in his arms and a fire to keep them warm, and he realized he'd found a home. *If she lets me stay.*

"I want to ask you something." He didn't want to disturb their cozy connection, but his Firebird shifted under his skin with unease.

"What?" Estelle tilted her head to look at him.

"You have a new home and a new studio, and I'm sure you'll get a boatload of insurance money from the building that burned." He rubbed her hands with his. "It seems like your holidays and your future are going in the right direction."

"Yeah, I can see that." She squeezed his hand. "Is that okay?"

"Of course. I want the best for you."

"But?" She raised her eyebrows.

"But I also want to be in it with you." He grimaced as he let his gaze rest on the flames behind the fire grate. "I want to spend as much time with you as you'll allow. Especially alone." He hugged her a moment. "Would you mind if I stayed here with you when I'm not working?"

She pulled out of his arms and turned to face him. "Would I mind? Not at all. I'd like you to be here." She tilted her head and shot him a shy smile. "In fact, I'd like you to be here as much as possible."

"What does that mean?" His heart thundered, but he didn't dare hope she meant move in.

She shrugged. "The way I figure it, my uncle gave this house to me and to you as a way to make a home for both of us. He knows you live at the fire station and don't have your own place. Maybe he thought this would help us both."

"The house and land are definitely in your name, Estelle. I'd never claim it as mine."

"I know, and that's good." She nodded with a sweet smile. "But in the meantime, maybe you and I can make it into more than just a place to live. I'd like to make it a home. With you."

Excitement ran rampant through him, but he tried to rein it in. "Are you sure? I don't want to pressure you into anything." He grinned when she rolled her eyes. "But I definitely want to take you up on your offer."

"Then do it. I want to be with you, Mark. You've

already said we're bound together. I'd like you to be here when you can." She turned her head and gestured to the windows overlooking the snowy expanse of the backyard. "And there's plenty of open space with no neighbors here when you need to shift into your fiery self. It would be safe for both of us." She returned her gaze to his. "What do you say?"

"I say yes. I want to make my home here with you."

A brilliant grin split her face and he reveled in all the heat and love she offered. "Thank goodness!"

He laughed as she threw herself into his arms. "Did you think I'd say no?"

"I wasn't sure. I was worried you'd go all polite on me and insist you couldn't intrude or something." She pulled back and kissed him. "I love you, *hookesiteeno.*"

"I love you, too, *beebeenei.* And I love it when you call me that."

"What, Little Fire?"

"Yeah." He grinned as he swore he heard his grandmother's laugh. Hohou, nei'eibehe'. *Thank you, Grandmother.*

"Okay, now we definitely need some cake." She pulled the plates she'd brought closer to her and used the pie server to cut the cake. "We have some celebrating to do."

She served them a large slice of chocolate with a candle in each. "Would you do the honors, please?"

He laughed and let a little of his Firebird come through, lighting the candles in a short burst. She grinned and handed him his plate.

"Don't forget to make a wish."

He laughed again as she closed her eyes, a sweet smile curling her lips. He watched her with delight. He didn't have to make a wish. He had his mate and a new home to settle. His Yuletide wish had already come true.

THE END

Author's Note:

BURNING YULETIDE belongs to the Warbler Peninsula series, but Mark Redfeather's twin brother, Thomas Redfeather, will get his own story in the Elemental Hearts series, which is connected to the Cloudburst Colorado series. So many characters of mine often overlap and you might see them showing up in unlikely places throughout all my stories. Keep your eyes peeled. Thank you for reading.

Siobhan

ORDER OF THE DRAGON
WARBLER PENINSULA, BOOK 1
SNEEK PEEK

Drake MacGregor always adhered to the adage 'let sleeping dragons lie', until he slept with one.

In an effort to make up for his past as Vlad the Impaler, Drake has been living a small, quiet life in Three Lakes. As the town's archivist, his knowledge of history and his place in it weigh on him. Drake has one desire—to rectify the atrocities committed in the name of his knightly order. Too bad he can't keep his hands, or his fangs, off the local doctor, especially when he discovers she's an actual dragon.

Aliandra Cantora del Viento is old enough and wise enough to ignore her attraction to the handsome historian, especially when her heart suggests he might be something more than he appears. Drake stokes her fires and curls her tail, and after a hot night in her clinic, the game is on. But he avoids her and nothing she tries breaks through his reserve, despite his obvious interest. He turns her on then apologizes for it, repeatedly. Not exactly the kind of relationship she'd hoped for yet she can't walk away.

When a mysterious researcher arrives with his son, Drake becomes more edgy and irritable, and Aliandra must decide if she's willing to fight for him. Especially when he might be her True Mate.

THE VALKYRIE'S SWORD
WARBLER PENINSULA, BOOK 2
SNEEK PEEK

Svanhild isn't looking for a new sword, even when one's handed to her...

Svanhild Bjørnsdottir doesn't need much—just a place to work in order to fix her Valkyrie motorcycle before moving on. As a fallen Valkyrie, she has no hope of settling down or returning to the Shield Maidens. Odin exiled her for defying him, and she's not interested in going back, especially after arriving at the Fix-It Cave in Three Lakes, Michigan. But the last thing she's looking for is love.

As a Blade in the fanatical Sword of God, a religious group bent on protecting humans from the Elder Races, Balder Templar is haunted by the ghost of his last target and his part in the deaths of her werewolf family. Hunting redemption and respite, his path leads him to Kate Blackamber, the *Morukai* shaman of Three Lakes. Kate knows who he is, what he's done, and what he needs.

The *Morukai* lays a geas on both Svanhild and Balder—to help the other become part of the community. But when Balder rescues a little girl from an apartment fire and is recognized for his past, packmembers of the ghost arrive to demand retribution. In a town that abhors the Sword of God, Balder doesn't have many defenders, but the Valkyrie may just be his saving grace.

OTHER BOOKS BY SIOBHAN MUIR

Cloudburst Colorado Series
A Hell Hound's Fire
The Beltane Witch
Christmas I.C.E. Magic
Cloudburst Ice Magic

Rifts Series
Take the Reins
A Centaur's Solstice Wish
In Death's Shadow

Bad Boys of Beta Squad Series
Bronco's Rough Ride
The Navy's Ghost
Rimshot's Hard Target (from Amazon KindleWorlds)
Bam-Bam's Inked Hart

The Ivory Road
A Walk in the Sand
Outback Dreams

Triple Star Ranch Series
Rope a Falling Star
Star Light, Star Bright

Warbler Peninsula Series
Order of the Dragon
The Valkyrie's Sword
Burning Yuletide

Current Stand-alones
Queen Bitch of the Callowwood Pack (from Three Lakes Books)
Second Chance Succubus (from Three Lakes Books)

Darwin's Evolution (from Amazon KindleWorlds)
Wildfire's Heart (from Three Lakes Books)
Her Devoted Vampire (from Three Lakes Books)

Coming Soon
Cloudburst Coffee &Spa
Courting the Dragon Widow
Deli's Take Out

ABOUT THE AUTHOR

Siobhan Muir lives in Cheyenne, Wyoming, with her husband, two daughters, and a vegetarian cat she swears is a shape-shifter, though he's never shifted when she can see him. When not writing, she can be found looking down a microscope at fossil fox teeth, pursuing her other love, paleontology. An avid reader of science fiction/fantasy, her husband gave her a paranormal romance for Christmas one year, and she was hooked for good.

In previous lives, Siobhan has been an actor at the Colorado Renaissance Festival, a field geologist in the Aleutian Islands, and restored inter-planetary imagery at the USGS. She's hiked to the top of Mount St. Helens and to the bottom of Meteor Crater.

Siobhan writes kick-ass adventure with hot sex for men and women to enjoy. She believes in happily ever after, redemption, and communication, all of which you will find in her paranormal romance stories.

Connect with Siobhan online at:
https://www.siobhanmuir.com
https://www.facebook.com/siobhan.muir.35
https://twitter.com/SiobhanMuir
https://www.siobhanmuir.com/siobhans-blog
https://pinterest.com/siobhanmuir35
https://tatsnteddys.tumblr.com

www.ingramcontent.com/pod-product-compliance
Lightning Source LLC
Chambersburg PA
CBHW072229190626
46809CB00017B/1541